TEMPERED GLASS

A COLLECTION OF SHORT STORIES

STACEY LONGO

MACEY MAE
PUBLISHING

Cover image by Stephanie Johnson sljohnsonimages.com

"Of Giraffes and Men" first appeared in *Carnival of Fear*, © 2018 Limitless Publishing
"Miss Elizabeth's Poison" first appeared in *My Peculiar Family*, © 2016 Sci Fi Saturday Night/Belanger Books
"Eat Your Vegetables" first appeared in *Insanity Tales III*, © 2017 Storyside Press
"The Devil's in the Details" first appeared in *Insanity Tales II*, © 2015 Books & Boos Press
"Early Evening on Leech Lake" first appeared in *VHS Nightmares*, © 2020 Danger Meows
"Color Him Crazy" first appeared in *Insanity Tales*, © 2014 Books & Boos Press
"Gibtown" first appeared in *Carnival of Nightmares*, © 2018 Limitless Publishing

Printed in the United States of America

ISBN: 978-0-9979274-7-4

For Matt

"Paul Stanley is my spirit animal."

CONTENTS

INTRODUCTION

Before I begin with this introduction, there's a rumor about Stacey Longo that I think is worth sharing. I've heard when Stacey was born, the doctor, per practice, held her up by the feet and gave her bum a little tap. Instead of crying, Stacey laughed. Her laugh was so infectious it had everyone in the hospital room doubled over. I believe that rumor. To this day, Stacey's good humor remains (with no tap on the bum required) and is evidenced in her work.

When I was a fledging writer and attending my inaugural horror convention in 2009, Stacey was the first person I met. Funny, warm, affable, I remember thinking that I hoped everyone else would be as welcoming and charming as she was. Even without knowing of her talent, I knew I had met a special person.

Our next meeting was at another convention a year or two later. By then, I realized Stacey was not only a recognizable horror author, but a respected editor as well. She was at a welcome desk handing out author copies of the New England Horror Writers collection called *Epitaphs*, an anthology I had a story in. Confused when she saw me, I explained my tale was written in a pen name. "You wrote 'The Old Man'?" she asked with a huge smile on her face. "I love that story!" Turned out, she had edited it. I returned her smile and wore it for the duration of the convention.

The third time we met sealed the deal for a lasting friendship. We were both attending a wedding for mutual friends, and we found ourselves spending quite a bit of time together. Fortified with a few beers, I proposed that we each write a novella, and submit them as a team. To my relief, Stacey didn't shoot me down. She loved the idea and then added that she would serve as publisher. Another writer came on board, and her publishing company released our three novellas as *Triplicity*. We attended signings together after *Triplicity* was released, and our friendship continued to grow.

Though Stacey and I have not worked together again up until now, we have remained in touch, sharing the good and bad events in our lives. When she asked me to write the introduction for *Tempered Glass*, I was delighted.

As I was reading this collection, I was reminded that Stacey excels at more than penning comedic dark fiction. When it comes to pathos, she has few peers who share her ability to generate touching, effective, and heartbreaking prose. *Tempered Glass* showcases Longo's talents in both those traits.

When it comes to comedic dark fantasy in *Tempered Glass*, Stacey shines in stories that will have you laughing out loud. Tales highlighting her ability to have a reader guffawing (or at least smiling broadly) include a woman trying awfully hard to lose weight ("Eat Your Vegetables"), a young woman who, at first, finds the bright side in being possessed ("The Devil's in the Details"), a tale of a girl who is hoping to hook up with a boy at the lake until things go terribly wrong ("Early Evening On Leech Lake"), a high-schooler whose greed allows her to experience that old adage *you get what you wish for* ("Popular"), and how bad a first date can go ("Andy Warhol Is My Wingman"). My favorite story in this collection hilariously chronicles the exploits of two friends who work at a local children's theme park and how their friendship is tested by a girl and a stuck zipper ("Of Giraffes and Men").

As for the pathos, when reading *Tempered Glass*, prepare to be gut-wrenched and your soul burdened. If you are prone to weeping, have a box of tissues nearby, you'll need them. Stacey introduces us to characters weighed down by issues of the heart and other problems, some of which are not all too common. A young girl, at her own risk, mixes potions for women in trouble, only to run across one woman whose motives for a potion are suspect ("Miss Elizabeth's Poison"). When a cheating man decides to go out to eat while his girlfriend is visiting a psychic but then gets something besides food on the side, he discovers his girlfriend isn't so clueless about his activities ("Hungry Man"). For Mariah, becoming mentally lost starts slowly, but when it accelerates, it leaves her shaken and confused, longing for a way out ("Down the Corridor of the Forgotten Mind"). You'll need the tissues for this one: a story of a woman dying and the list she creates that her and her husband attempt to complete before her passing ("Bucket List"). A point-of-view tale of the old west about a woman coerced to join her husband for a better life in California when they join the Donner-Reed expedition is amazing, bleak, and upsetting ("Winter Of My Discontent").

There are four more stories in *Tempered Glass* that don't fit snugly into Stacey's oeuvre. They straddle the line between darkly comic and poignancy, leaving the reader uncomfortable and musing on the frailties of the human condition. In one tale, a woman watches dispassionately as her husband becomes ill and deteriorates quickly ("Sick"). Another chronicles the life of a man who is born into a family of mentally unstable, violent killers, and he questions whether he suffers from the same affliction ("Color Him Crazy"). We meet a person who discovers that dog really is man's best friend, and the lengths they will go to ensure that friendship ("Free To Good Home"). Finally, in the highlight of the collection, we have a story of a woman investigating the disappearance of the owner of a traveling carnival, and the members of its freak show are her only chance at getting to the truth ("Gibtown").

I've read Stacey's long and short fiction for as long as I've known her, so I can say with confidence that *Tempered Glass* is her best release yet. She is a remarkable talent. Her prose is accessible and entertaining, rich in atmosphere and characterization, and it never fails to leave an impression. Whether it comes to dark comedic fantasy, horror, drama, or heartbreak, Stacey is at her very best in *Tempered Glass*. These stories are all so damn good.

Tony Tremblay
May 2023

"Tempered glass can withstand impacts . . . that would shatter laminated glass."

~ Peter Chen, *The Ultimate Guide to Toughened Glass*

SICK

He is sick. She knows this.

She knows this because he tells her every day. In the morning, he complains of a headache. She once foolishly suggested it was a hangover—after all, he polishes off a twelve-pack just about every night—and he called her an idiot. Told her she didn't get how alcohol worked. That the glass of water and two ibuprofen he took every night before bed cured all.

By midmorning he starts to grumble about his back. It's always his lower back, and it's always after he's been sitting in bed for three or four hours. She knows better than to suggest that his back pain might be from the awkward angle at which he props himself up on the pillows, peering at his computer and sipping the tea he demands she bring him.

After lunch, it's his stomach that bothers him. He can't have dairy—was there cream in the soup she served him? He has no tolerance for beans, and fats, and vegetables with skin. His sandwiches lack tomatoes and onions and condiments. She feeds him meat on dry bread and salty broth. No wonder he's miserable.

As she folds the laundry and dusts the light fixtures in the midafternoon, he calls out to her that he can't sleep with all of her bustling. He needs the room dark, and the house silent. He must nap to make up for the restless insomnia he suffers most nights.

By evening, he doesn't want to eat. His stomach is still too topsy-turvy. A cold Pabst Blue Ribbon will do the trick, he says. Then another. Then a third. He's remarkably sprightly after the third. Climbing up and down the stairs himself, and his backache and migraine and delicate stomach are miraculously cured. He's loud and belligerent and affectionate and randy. She shudders at his touch.

She likes him better sick.

It's why she's been poisoning him.

OF GIRAFFES AND MEN

"**T**en ninja shifts in a *row*, man—fist bump!"

Roland and Dwight tapped fists, laughing as they strolled back to the cast locker rooms at Grilligan's Island. It had been an easy day—the costumes were first come, first served, and they'd gotten to work early yet again, scoring the white cotton outfits of Suki and Yaki, the hibachi ninja twins, easily the most coveted costumes among the cast member staff. They were lightweight and cool, and as a bonus making them even more desirable, the characters didn't have to talk. Roland cast an empathetic eye toward Hank Hannigan, who'd shown up that morning two minutes before the park opened, and was now red-faced and sweating as he wrested the fifteen-pound head of Giggles the Giraffe off his shoulders.

"Great job out there today, everyone!" Their supervisor, a graying, burly man everyone called the Skipper, clapped each performer on the back as they filtered into the locker room. "Only four reports of crying tots—remember, whoever is playing the lobster, try not to hold your claws like you're about to gut the kiddies—and only one fainter. Sounds like a win to me!"

"I had one overeager dad pick me up and shake me," complained one of the Marilyn Monroe impersonators. "I think he cracked one of my ribs."

"Suck it up, Marilyn," the Skipper said. "I will *not* be entertaining workers' comp claims this early in the season."

Grilligan's was the most popular amusement park/hibachi grill destination in central North Carolina, and Roland knew guys his age from all over Chatham County who tried every year to get on staff. The pay was great, though the hours long, particularly if one was working a vending kiosk selling fried funnel cakes in the sweltering summer heat, or cleaning up spilled soda and spraying for bees around the grounds—or worst of all, fishing out turd floaters at the Wet Dreams Lazy River Ride. But this was Roland's and Dwight's third season at Grilligan's, and this year they'd been promoted to the most coveted positions of all: character cast.

The shifts were cake: sure, it was twenty minutes in stifling costumes, letting children crawl all over you, handing out balloons and sometimes, if the mascot you'd gotten stuck with was a *talkie*, having to learn and repeat stupid park slogans. But then cast members got forty minutes of downtime every hour to relax, cool off, maybe flirt with the Marilyns from the Hollywood Starlet Revue show. It was a sweet gig, and Roland expected to make more than enough to finance his textbooks and late-night pizzas for his upcoming senior year at Duke.

Dwight, his best bud, was a natural at play-acting park characters—much more so than Roland, who still tripped over Pineapple Shrimp Sally's "Tanga-ranga-licious!" catch phrase—and left every photo op with a line of giggling kids trailing him, and on more than one occasion, their big sister's or mother's phone number, too. Hell, he'd already slept with both Marilyns, and it was still only June. It wasn't just Dwight's thick black hair, deep dimples and quick smile that charmed the ladies. There was something about him, something magnetic, which made guys want to hang around him, and women to shed their clothes for him.

Roland was not so lucky with the ladies. He was rail-thin and had never grown into his gangly stature, hunching over and cringing whenever anyone asked him if he played basketball, a question he got daily at the park. He had never once even shot a basket, stubbornly refusing to give in to the stereotype. On top of this, he had an angry red rash of acne along his jawline, and after trying every possible remedy, from Proactiv to smearing toothpaste on his cheeks, had finally given up and started growing a beard. In June. Working one of the sweatiest jobs in central North Carolina.

Coming in nicely, though, Roland thought, running the back of his hand along the reddish bristles. Maybe in a couple weeks, when it was a little thicker, he'd finally feel confident enough to make the effort to flirt with Allie, one of the mermaids at Wet Dreams.

He'd first met her at OSHA training, one of those mandatory classes all the staff had to sit through at the beginning of the season. He'd cursed his rotten luck that he'd been scheduled for early morning training, while ever-lucky Dwight had scored the late afternoon classes, which would give him plenty of time to sleep off his hangover. But when the smoking-hot redhead had slid into the empty seat next to Roland's, he'd changed his tune.

It was her first year at Grilligan's, and she knew no one, so he'd been happy to offer his assistance. "You know, if you need someone to show you the ropes—which vendors will sneak you free hibachi dogs, where the cleanest bathrooms are . . ." She was smiling politely. He was losing her. "So you're a mermaid? Which one?"

The mermaids didn't have to follow the same rules as the rest of the cast members. They were assigned outfits at the start of the season, and if you were Conch on Memorial Day, you were guaranteed to still be wearing a giant seashell in your hair on Labor Day. "Starfish," she said. "Definitely the best bra—you know, the most coverage up top—but those stupid headpieces!" Each mermaid had to fashion their locks into a bun every morning, and attach an elaborate, ungainly barrette in the shape of their assigned character. Some joker years ago had cut the things out of twenty-two-gauge sheet metal and spray-painted them a variety of florescent colors with sparkles. They were heavy and had lots of pointy bits, and many a mermaid had complained of spraining their necks fastening the things. The starfish topper was bright orange with blue glitter, an array of stabby sea arms spread across the back of the head.

"Rotten luck. Cut yourself yet?"

"Twice." She grinned, holding up two Band-Aided fingers, and his heart had tapped out a tango. "Oh, look—there's Jellyfish! It was nice meeting you, Ronald." She switched seats, breaking his heart, and was soon giggling with a brunette mermaid two tables over.

It was too late. He'd fallen in love. Hard.

"Earth to Roland?" Dwight snapped his fingers in front of Roland's face, making him flinch. "C'mon, man, let's grab some grub." Dwight was already out of his Yaki garb, looking chill in a Duke tee and cutoffs. "The all-you-can-eat peppercorn steak poppers only goes on for another fifteen."

Employees got free meals, but serving times and locations were limited to management's whims. Thursdays, the staff dinner was from 6:30 to 7:15 at the Professor's Coconut Hibachi Hut, on the other side of the grounds, near the Volcanic Drop. They'd have to hurry.

Roland pulled his shirt on as Dwight tugged him along through the park. They broke into a jog as they got closer and saw the line; peppercorn popper Thursdays were *very* popular among the employees. Once in line, Roland bent over, hands on knees, to catch his breath.

"Dude." Dwight giggled. "Nice hair."

"Really?"

"No. You look like Miley Cyrus lost a fight with a porcupine."

Roland glared at his friend, spat into his palms, and tried to slick down his cowlick. "Better?"

"Uh, sure. Well hel-*lo* there." Dwight shifted to face the woman behind them, and Roland followed his gaze. *Allie.*

She wore a pink tank top that showed off her bronzed skin, and Roland wondered for a minute how the heck she had no tan lines, what with sitting in a starfish bra all day on a rock in the water park. He let his eyes glaze over trying to picture how she'd accomplished that—but no, he had to focus. He hadn't told Dwight of his little crush, and Roland knew better than anyone how easily Dwight could melt even the iciest women to puddles with just a wink and a flash of those dimples. Even his greeting to Allie had been smooth as warm honey, delivered with just the right combination of lackadaisical and lothario. Roland held his breath waiting for her response.

"Hi."

That hi—she'd very distinctly looked at *both* of them as she said it, and had Roland detected a hint of—curiosity? Excitement? Dare he dream it—*interest*, in that hi? Was it possible she was the one female on the planet impervious to Dwight's charms? He couldn't pooch this one. *Be cool, man. Indifferent, yet intriguing. This is your shot.*

"Yo!" he answered, then cringed. "I mean, hi—right back at'cha."

Allie's perfectly plucked brows furrowed. She hated him. He just knew it.

"You're funny," she finally announced.

Hot damn!

She sat with them for dinner, she and Dwight laughing as they exchanged inappropriate adult behavior stories and described the worst kids they'd ever borne witness to. *You're funny*, Roland replayed over and over in his mind, smiling and nodding and trying desperately to think of something— anything—witty to add.

"So then the ankle biter line-jumps *again*, and I knew we'd just had a kid blow chunks going down the water slide. I should've called it in, I know—I mean, it was obvious, there were barfed-up corn dog lumps all over the entrance to the pipe. But that little brat didn't even really give me a chance, I swear. He just elbowed past the other kids—half of them were still crying over the puke, you think the line-jumper would've noticed, but no, he dove face-first and got a mouthful of the Sick and Slide. Best day I've had all summer," Allie finished, a wistful smile playing across her lips.

"Upchucklehead," Roland said brightly, sure he had a winner.

Dwight and Allie turned to him, unsmiling.

"Dude, that's like, a joke my grandpa would make." Dwight shook his head.

"Sorry," Roland muttered.

It was not lost on him that it was Dwight's hand she touched when she asked, "You guys wanna go on some rides?"

They hit the Meteor Whirl first, the three of them cramming into one bench seat. Roland moved to drape his arm across the back, and by default around Allie, but encountered Dwight's arm already there when he tried. He tried to lock eyes with his friend, send him a telepathic *I'm into her, man, back off*, but Dwight was too busy whispering in Allie's ear to notice. This was not going well at all.

Next up was the pirate ship, and when Roland tried to step into the same seat with the other two, Allie looked at him apologetically: "I don't think there's enough room. Sorry." He slid into the row behind them, shoulders slumping as he was once again delegated to the role he knew so well: third wheel. But then when they got off the ride after being sling-shot on a pendulum, Allie put one hand on his arm, the other on her belly as she moaned, "Now I know why so many people get sick on that thing!"

Roland's arm was on fire where she touched him, and his heart soared.

It was well after closing when the trio left Grilligan's. "I'm in Lot B," Allie said, and Roland's heart sank. Dwight was parked there, too.

"I'm in C. Dwight—can I talk to you for a sec?"

Dwight shrugged. "What, bro?"

"About the morning. I'm still picking you up, right?" Dwight had an appointment to drop off his car for body detailing before work.

"Sure, man." He stepped closer—*finally*.

Roland swallowed hard and let his voice drop. "Don't hook up with her, okay? I mean, you can have any chick in the park. Just—not her." His cheeks burned with humiliation. Having to beg his effortlessly charismatic friend to not score with the girl he had a crush on . . . this was definitely one of the lowest points in his life. "I really like her," he added. This was mortifying. Could he sound more like a whiny baby?

Dwight's grin flashed under the parking lot's light pole. "Seriously?" Roland scowled, and Dwight held up a palm. "Okay, yeah, I see you are. No worries. Compadres before madres, right? I'd never. Hand to God." He raised a palm, then clapped Roland's shoulder. "Relax. I'll dial the charm down to minimum." He grinned, green eyes flashing, then strolled toward Allie, calling back, "See you at six?"

"See you then," Roland said, relieved.

Roland tossed and turned that night. *You're funny*, she'd said. But it was Dwight's elbow she'd grabbed during the Haunted Natives' Village Ride; Dwight who she'd leaned into on the Meteor Whirl, and what had that whispering been about? But his best buddy had promised: compadres before madres.

His Accord idled at Big Bruce's Body Shop for over thirty minutes before Dwight pulled in, tires squealing. "I overslept," he explained, clambering into Roland's car.

Roland took in his friend—hair tumbled, eyes red, the faint odor of stale beer filling the front seat. "Late night?" he asked, stomach clenching as he waited for the answer.

"WiFi went down again. Ma had me outside with a flashlight looking for loose wires, and I'd had a couple Heinies before she even asked, so it took a while." Dwight popped the lid on the coffee Roland handed him. "Thanks, man. You're the best."

"We're gonna be late," Roland said. Christ, even he couldn't stand the whine in his own voice.

"So we're not the ninjas. It's just one day. Streak had to end sometime," Dwight said with a shrug. "Ugh. My stomach's been acting up since the poppers last night. You feeling okay?"

"Fine," Roland said, but he didn't think he'd eaten much at dinner anyway. "Maybe it's just a bug. If we see Allie today, we can ask her if she's . . ."

"Nah, I'm sure you're right—a bug." Roland's heart soared at Dwight's dismissal. Clearly, he had no interest in flirting with the beautiful mermaid again, but this certainly gave Roland an opening to seek her out. He hummed along to the radio as he drove, pausing only to point out the can of Febreze in the back seat, in case Dwight wanted to freshen up.

They parked in the last spot left in B and sprinted to the locker room, slowing only to flash their employee badges to security as they ran through the gates. *There might still be time*, Roland thought. *We might still get Luther the Lobster—*

coveted because the bottom half of Luther was red tights, much less sweat-inducing than a full-body fur costume. But no; when the boys arrived to the suit-up room, only two remained: Penny the Panda and Giggles, the heavy, bulky, sweat-stinking, gag-inducing giraffe.

Roland's shoulders slumped. He knew how this would go. There was no way Dwight wasn't going to nab the panda, had every right to demand it just by nature of being infinitely cooler—

"You okay with Penny?"

Roland's head shot up. "Hell yeah," he said, grabbing the black-and-white oversized cartoon head before Dwight could take back what he'd just said. "Seriously?" he added guiltily.

"I could ask you the same thing. You really okay with being a chick?"

"Wait; what?" Dwight didn't want the Penny outfit because she was a—a girl? In today's gender-fluid day and age, and who the hell would be able to *tell* under the fleece, anyway, if it was a man or a woman donning the fur? Plus, to sweeten the costume choice even further, Penny Panda didn't speak. Not one *tanga-ranga-licious*, no *ooh, that's tempura-tempting!* Besides the sweatbox of the costume, Giggles the Giraffe also had a stupid *hee-hoo-ho* guffaw that made Roland die a little inside each time they practiced it in their cast meetings. *I'd rather be a female character than stuck in a costume that reeks of sweaty ball sacks, laughing like a mental ward escapee all day,* he wanted to say. "I'm fine being a girl. Knock yourself out," he offered instead, and Dwight scooped up the giraffe costume, practicing the Giggles giggle as he shuffled into the bathroom to change.

Roland shook his head. Dwight might be all that and a bag of Fritos, but if that meant passing on the panda in favor of Giggles, Roland was just fine with being the dork of the duo today.

Their first twenty-minute appearance was low energy. There was only a handful of people in the park that early, and the Marilyns were serving coconut tempura flapjacks at the Hollywood Canteen, which always drew a crowd. Roland hung back a minute while Dwight, still in full giraffe garb, managed to charm what appeared to be a teenage mom with twins into texting him her digits. *Unbelievable. She can't even see those dimples through the neck hole, and he's still got her eating out of his palm.* Roland shook his giant panda head and headed back to the locker room solo. The sweat had already soaked through his shirt, and the day promised to only get hotter.

Dwight popped in with just ten minutes to go before the next mascot appearance, this time over in Tiny Town. They had to duck onto the employees-only path behind the tall fence running the perimeter of the park, a trail running through a maze of trees that all the costumed cast used to get from one end of Grilligan's to the other quickly without getting stopped by eager children looking for free balloons. "Dude, this giraffe smells like the inside of a dumpster filled with jock straps," Dwight complained.

"Too late to switch," Roland said gleefully.

Twenty more minutes in the hot sun. The Tiny Town crowd was bigger, but not bad: only two crying babies and one big brother threatening to give his sister a black eye if she didn't hand over the last green balloon. Dwight didn't stay to flirt this time; he hustled over to Roland on polka-dotted giraffe legs as soon as Sally Shrimp announced it was time to tanga-ranga-toodle-loo. "Bro, come with me. I hafta take a dump, and I'm gonna need help getting out of the costume."

"Gee, that's *so* tempting. No thanks."

"I'm serious, man. It's an emergency. My stomach's killing me, and the Skipper's head will pop off his neck if I get molten lava squirts all over the costume. Just come with me to the back john."

The back john was an old tin one-seater bathroom behind Tiny Town, located on a side trail off the employees-only path. It was still operational, but disgusting: the cleaning staff never bothered to stop in there, and as a result, it collected all sorts of goodies over the course of the season: garbage, spider webs, and the distinct aroma of unflushed sewage.

"That bad, huh?" If Dwight wanted to stop at the back john, then yeah, it was an emergency.

The two ducked behind the fence, Dwight moving at a full trot. A wall of stink greeted Roland when he pulled off his panda head inside neglected hut. He swallowed back the urge to gag.

"I can't—dude—can't reach the zipper." Dwight squirmed, hands behind his neck in a ridiculous pantomime that made Roland think of a chicken.

"Hold on. I'll get it." He pulled his T-shirt up over his nose, preferring the rapidly increasing stink of his own body odor to the stench of the back john.

The zipper firmly securing the giraffe head to the body suit wouldn't budge. Roland gave it a stronger tug. Nothing. "There's a tooth not lined up or something," he muttered. He looked around, spotted a capless pen on the floor, and scooped it up, sticking it into the zipper tab for more leverage. He yanked again.

Snap.

"What was that? Did the pen break?"

"Uh . . . no. The tab just broke off the zipper." Roland cringed at the string of cuss words pouring out of Dwight, but he couldn't blame him.

"Get—me—out—of—this—thing! Now!"

"I'm *working* on it!" Roland left his friend sitting on a dirty blue bench to rummage for something that would help—pliers, maybe. The back john consisted of two rooms—a front open area, so small it only housed a couple of lockers, the bench, and an overflowing garbage can, which from one whiff Roland could tell had been put into service some time ago as a urinal. This didn't deter the yellow jackets from buzzing about it, however: their low drone could be heard even from the back room, which housed a toilet, sink, and medicine cabinet. Roland opened this, hoping for something—nail file?—that might be put into service.

"Hurry up," Dwight called. "It's gotta be a hundred degrees in this dumb giraffe!"

Not much cooler out of the fur—indeed, the tin roof of the back john had rendered the stuffy hut an oven, but Roland kept silent. The cobwebbed, sticky shelves of the medicine cabinet were empty, save for—"Hey, man, come look at this!"

Dwight appeared at the doorway, one hoof between his legs, like a child in desperate need of a potty break. "What?"

"Look."

"Better be a set of wire cutters," he grumbled, joining Roland at the cabinet. "What is it?"

"Is that a black widow?" Roland said, fascinated. The spider, hanging motionless on fine gossamer strands, was shiny black, legs longer and body plumper than he'd imagined. Sure, he'd seen the pictures in the brochures the parks and rec department distributed every year, but he'd never encountered one for real, in the wild—

Splat.

"Not anymore." Dwight wiped a cloven paw on his polka-dot thigh.

"You're a real asshole, you know that?"

"It's two hundred degrees in here, I'm dizzy, and I'm clenching my sphincter so tight right now I'm worried I'm gonna suck this whole stinkin' giraffe outfit up my colon. I'm the asshole? Get me *out* of this thing!"

"Sorry, man. You're right. Nothing in here." He closed the mirrored door. "I'll check the lockers."

Nothing, but as Roland scooped out empty beer cans, an idea struck him. "My pocketknife!"

"You been holding out?" Dwight's hoofs curled into fists, but he was slumping on the bench now, and it sounded like he was panting. Roland doubted the guy had the energy to land a serious punch.

"It's not on me—it's back in the cast lockers. You wanna come with, or wait here while I go get it?"

"I'll wait. But hurry up, man. And could you bring back some water?"

Roland jogged, then slowed to a walk as he headed through the wooded path to the locker room. It really was sweltering out, probably pushing up over ninety degrees already. As he slid his Penny face out from under his arm and over his head, he ducked through the wooden gate into the main park.

"Pen Pan!" a toddler lisped, pointing. "Pen Pan!"

Not now, kid, he thought, but if he didn't stop and do a little dance and wave, he might get reported to management and lose his job. He obliged the kid with a shuffle-step, then moved on, waving as he scampered to the cast room. It was mostly empty, save one Marilyn blowing smoke circles by the back door. Where was everyone? He glanced at his watch. Seven minutes 'til the next appearance. *Oh no.*

He threw open his locker, rummaging through his backpack until he found the silver-plated pocketknife his dad had given him for Christmas a few years back. Roland had been hoping for a car, but had thanked his father profusely anyway, not wanting to seem like an ingrate. "Most important tool a man can have," his father had pronounced.

Until this very moment, Roland had not once used the Boy Scout knife for anything more important than cleaning out the dirt under his fingernails.

He unzipped his suit, sliding the knife in his shorts pocket before pulling the zipper back up—and, thinking guiltily of the overheated giraffe in the back john, leaving the slider an inch or so from the top so it wouldn't get stuck. Then he hurried over to the stage outside Howell Caverns for the next photo op.

Twenty minutes later—felt like forever, and he was sweating like a pig!—he stopped at the Tourist Trap souvenir shop, paid for a water, and made his way back to Dwight, shedding the panda suit outside the hut. Really, he didn't know how Dwight could stand it.

"Show-off," Dwight said weakly when Roland entered in his tee and shorts. "Nice legs, though."

"Shut up. We'll get you out of this thing soon enough. Sorry it took so long—had to make a pit stop to do the Howell Hibachi-cha-cha." He handed Dwight the water, then flipped open the knife.

Dwight struggled with the cap on the water, his gloved hands sliding over the plastic to no effect, then handed it back to Roland in defeat.

"Sorry." One twist, and he handed it back. Dwight held the bottle up to the mesh screen that formed a black circle in Giggles's throat to allow the cast member inside to breathe. He tilted the bottle and sputtered.

"C'mon now! Not that the water doesn't feel good, but I'm so thirsty . . . can you start by sawing through the mesh? I'm dying here!"

"I thought you needed the bathroom?" Roland eyed the zipper at the back of Dwight's neck.

"It passed. Trust me—water's the priority now. I'm so dehydrated I thought you were one of the Marilyns when you came back in. I'm hallucinating, man." There was an edge of fear to Dwight's tone, and goose bumps crept up Roland's arms despite the heat. He suspected his friend wasn't kidding. The *nice legs* comment hadn't been like him at all.

He sat next to the giraffe, eyeing the mesh. It looked metal, not plastic, confirmed when he made a tentative poke. *Gonna take some time*, he thought, but didn't share. He started sawing.

"Careful—that's my face!" Dwight flinched as the knife slipped, sinking deeper than Roland had intended.

"Sorry. Try to lean back, okay?" Roland tried to make shallower slices, but found he was getting nowhere. *Penny the Panda might be noticeably absent for the next photo op.* He paused to wipe away the sweat dripping into his eyes, then took a swig of Dwight's water.

"I'll kill you if you do that again." Through the mesh, Dwight's eyes were angry black coals.

Roland mumbled an apology and went back to work with renewed vigor. The faster he got through this, the better.

Slowly, little metal filigrees began to fall away. Roland had two stems cut, and was halfway through a third. The yellow jackets continued their buzzing, oblivious to the crisis on the bench.

Roland heard it before he saw it, and there was no time to react. He'd always hated the way Dwight sneezed—a loud, dramatic *waah-hooooie!* like a bad stage actor. Roland suspected he did this for attention more than anything else. Nobody sneezed that hard.

But this time, the sneeze was only halfway out—a *waaaa* as Dwight pulled back, but Roland had been pushing forward on this cut, and the *hooooie* was replaced by a screaming wail that turned Roland's veins to ice and made him scream in reply. He'd heard such a noise only once before, when a neighborhood cat was being ripped apart by coyotes in the field near his house, and it made his eardrums throb a painful beat just to hear it. "Wait, wait, what happened?"

But he could see what was going on—from the ooze and the shrieks and the knife that looked like it was suddenly missing half an inch of its tip. When Dwight ricocheted forward for the second half of his stupid sneeze, he'd impaled his left eye on the knife blade.

Roland thought he might throw up. He closed his eyes, breathing deeply, trying to remember if the eyeball was that vital of an organ. Yes, of course this was unpleasant and gross as hell, but not life threatening, right? Heatstroke was more of a worry at this point. He calmed himself by thinking of all the people he knew with only one eye: Nick Fury, Fetty Wap, that hot chick from *Kill Bill*. He scowled. Dwight with an eye patch would probably be a thousand times more popular with the ladies.

Dwight's illegible howl eventually softened to hitching little hiccups. It took a long time.

More than anything else, Roland really wanted to check his watch. He must've missed his next appearance, which would earn him a warning from the Skipper—his first ever.

Roland swallowed hard. "Let me take a look, man."

Dwight gave a little "uunh" and pulled back, separating eye from blade with a sickening pop. His snapped his eye shut. Even through the dark mesh, Roland could see jelly-like tears tinged with blood weeping from the lashes.

"I'm getting medical." Roland stood.

"No! You can't," Dwight said, his voice stronger—and more terrified—than it had been since the tab had first broken off the zipper. "Don't get anyone! *You* gotta help me."

"Dude, I'm not gonna lie—your eyeball doesn't look good at all, and that's without me even seeing the whole thing. I can't take care of that. I cheated off Hank Hannigan when we had to take that first aid exam at the start of the season." Roland paused. "What's that smell?"

"That's what I'm saying, man. You can't let anyone see me like this. I crapped myself. Just a little bit," he added defensively.

"Gross, dude."

"*You* get a knife in the eye and tell me you wouldn't squirt your drawers!" Dwight sounded indignant.

"Sorry—you're right. Listen, I'm sure medical's used to that stuff. They deal with sick kids in the park all day. You *know* those little brats are puking and pooping all the time." He moved toward the door. "I'll be back with an EMT in five."

"No! I'm also practically naked."

Roland hesitated in the doorway. "Huh?"

"It was so hot this morning, I . . . I stripped down. To the drawers."

T-shirts and shorts were required inside the suit. But doffing down—even going commando—was not unheard of, and most guys who got caught were simply demoted to the cotton candy kiosk for a week or so. "Big deal. So you're coated in spun sugar for a week. Dude, your *eye*." He stepped outside, marveling that the sticky humid air could actually feel cool after being inside the back john.

"It's not my underwear."

Roland turned back to look through the doorway. "What?"

"I'm not—you can't get medical in here. I'm wearing Allie's panties. They can't see that."

Spots of crimson filled Roland's vision—*so that's what they mean by seeing red*, a voice inside his head whispered, cold and reptilian. His jaw clenched. The whole thing: the "compadres before madres, hand to God" speech from the night before, the assurances this morning that Dwight had been up late looking for a downed Wi-Fi cable—*dude used his mother as a cover, how low can you go?* the voice hissed in his brain—all total BS.

"Would you care to elaborate?" Roland's words were clipped, his nails digging into his palms. *I'll kill you*, Dwight had said about the water. Roland snorted.

"Listen—I'm so sorry, man. It just happened. She was like a cat in heat—I couldn't have stopped her if I'd wanted to! I mean, I did want to, of course. Out of respect for you. But she— I walked her to her car, and she just grabbed my junk out of nowhere. And, you know, it felt good. Real good. I mean, it's been a few days, and a guy's got needs, right? So, yeah, I'm sorry. She gave me a hummer right there by the car. If it's any consolation"—he sat up straighter, the giraffe's neck pointing taller—"worst head I ever got in my life. Hands down."

"So," Roland spoke slowly, "she went down on you and you . . . took her panties?"

"Well, no, not then. She got all whiny and complainy about how she had needs too, all that crap, and, well, we went back to her place so she could get *her* rocks off. Then this morning after I nailed her again she made me put 'em on. Said it would be all sexy, thinking about me in her underwear." Dwight grunted. "The girl's really high maintenance. I actually did you a favor. She's a nut job. You're better off without her, I'm tellin' ya. You should be thanking me."

Roland opened his mouth to speak, then snapped it closed again. What could he say? *Anyone but her,* he'd begged, shaming himself at his desperation. Not so much to ask, he thought, of a friend, his *best* friend at this park three years running now, and Dwight had witnessed every one of Roland's miserable, failed attempts to pick up girls, any girl, heck, even to get one to agree to go for a soda with him at the Coconut Hut. It was Dwight who'd suggested he grow the beard to hide his inflamed pimples. How grateful Roland had been for the encouragement. *I'll bet you'd look sharp with a goatee,* Dwight had said. And Roland had followed the advice blindly, dumbly, so thankful to get just one nugget of wisdom from Mr. Steal Your Girl.

How stupid he'd been.

Roland spun on his heel, stalking away from the hut. He paused only to look at the collapsed panda suit, scooping it up as he made his way back into the park.

He made his next scheduled appearance.

He marveled at his own calm demeanor, feeling like an observer, hovering just above his own body, impressed by the delight with which Penny Panda greeted the tykes, pulling them on her lap and posing for the camera. Patting them on the head with a soft paw before sending them on their way. Even miming an elaborate drumroll before Pineapple Shrimp Sally gave an exuberant "Tanga-ranga-licious!"

What he purposely did not do was think about Dwight—or Allie—for the entire twenty minutes, pushing all thoughts aside when the reptilian voice threatened to slither in.

Until he got back to the locker room.

"Dwight? You here?"

He heard Allie before he saw her, and when she peeped around the corner, locking eyes with him, at least she had the decency to blush. "Oh, hi, Roland. Where's my bae?"

"Your? Your . . . Dwight. He's, uh . . . not feeling well. Say, you feeling okay? He's had an upset stomach since the poppers last night." There. It wasn't quite how he'd envisioned the opening with Allie, but at least he got to talk to her without sounding stupid.

"Oh, no! I mean, I'm fine. Poor baby! Where is he?"

"On the crapper. You do *not* want to go in there." Roland jerked a thumb toward the bathrooms.

"Listen," Allie said softly, taking a seat on the bench next to him. "I hope it's okay—I mean, that you're not upset—about me and Dwight. He told me you had the hots for me, and that's sweet and all, but . . . look, you're a nice guy. But Dwight and I are in a relationship now." She leaned forward, and Roland had a clear view down the spiked starfish neckline of her mermaid top. *Dwight was just admiring those in the flesh, what? Twelve hours ago?*

A twinge of guilt made his heart flutter, which surprised him. He thought only Allie had the power to make that happen, but his mind now returned to sanity, full-force focused on his friend, sweating and panicking with his eyeball leaking down his face in the back john. Maybe even dying. He shot to his feet.

"Noworriesgottagobye," he blurted, snatching the panda head off the bench before making his way to the woodsy path, stopping only to grab a cupful of ice and a straw from the soda vendor.

Dwight was lying flat on his back on the floor when Roland returned. "Hey, baby," he said, a little slurry. "Wanna sit on Giggles's lap? My neck ain't the only thing thass long, if you get my drift."

"A lobotomized chimpanzee would get your drift, bozo. Here." He pulled Dwight to a sitting position, then got his arms around his waist and lift-dragged him to the bench. He poured the water from the bottle he'd brought earlier—Christ, it was already hot as coffee—over the ice, stuck the straw in, and worked it through the hole he'd pried in the mesh earlier.

Dwight sucked eagerly.

"Don't think I'm not still super mad," Roland said, holding the cup. "You're truly the worst possible friend a guy could have."

"I *said* I was sorry, Marilyn." *Slurp-slurp.* "She meant nothin'. You know I only have eyes for you."

"Well, Romeo, you got some explaining to do then. 'Cause I just saw Allie, and she definitely doesn't think it meant nothing."

"Ooh—they should do that! Add a Romeo to the Hollywood Revue. I'd be s-o-o good at that," Dwight said. He squinted his good eye through the mesh. "Roland?"

"Yeah. Sorry. I know you were hoping for a naked starlet or something." Roland eyed the room. The overflowing garbage can was now on its side, trash littering the floor, yellow jackets skimming from piece to piece. "What happened here?"

Dwight took another long sip, then burped. "I'm dyin', man. I was looking for something to help rip through this dumb costume. Managed to work a hole in this arm with a beer tab"—he held up his left hoof, revealing a dime-sized tear—"but it's at a weird angle. Then a bee stung me right through the hole, the little jerk. What were you saying, that thing about Allie? You saw her?"

"Yup. She came over to the cast room looking for you. Oh, excuse me—looking for her *bae*."

Dwight groaned. "You're kidding, right?"

"I am not." Roland felt his ears growing hot.

"Dude, it was a hookup—nothing more. Did she sound like she was joking?"

"She certainly didn't. In fact, she gave me a whole friend-zone speech about how you two are in a relationship now, and she hopes my feelings aren't hurt, yada yada yada."

"She's nuts. I'm telling you, man. Completely off her rocker. Did I not mention the terrible head?" Giggles's head shook. "Awk-*ward*. Well, I'll just . . . pretend it never happened."

"You want to gaslight her?"

"Yeah—you with me? Just, like, if she brings up last night, dinner at the Coconut Hut, just act like you have no idea what she's talking about. You know."

"You want to gaslight her, and you want me to help." The reptile inside spoke this time, words so cold they chilled the air between them.

"Dude, what's your *problem*?" Dwight stood, wobbled, then sat again. "Can we shut up about that bang hole now and get me out of this thing? My whole face is throbbing, and my butt cheeks are starting to chafe."

Roland's hand slipped in his pocket, letting one finger slide along the cool handle of the knife. He stepped behind Dwight, brought it out, and studied the seam at the back of Dwight's neck. How easy it would be, to bury the blade into Dwight's spine right now, under the pretense of trying to slice open the costume.

Too easy, the serpent inside hissed. *You'd get caught.*

Roland nodded without realizing. This was true: if ever a more hapless, average, born-to-get-caught guy ever existed, Roland had yet to hear of him. Even the first aid exam—if he hadn't thought at the last minute to go back and change a couple answers so his responses wouldn't exactly match Hank's, he had no doubt he would've been busted for cheating. He sighed.

The loudspeaker system, the one running throughout the grounds of Grilligan's that was usually reserved for announcing show times and special deals on season passes throughout the day, chirped to life: "Giggles the Giraffe, please report to Tiny Town immediately." The speaker sounded cheerful, but it was the casting director giving the order, and both boys knew if there was one rule at Grilligan's to be followed above all else, it was *obey your skipper.*

"What's that about?" Dwight sounded nervous.

"You've missed, like, two appearances so far. Maybe three. I'm guessing he's ticked off about it."

"I can't go out there like this. I didn't want to say anything, but I peed myself a little, too."

"You're disgusting, you know that?"

"I know, I know. I can think of three homeless guys living under the James Taylor Bridge who smell prettier than me right now. That's what I'm saying. If I go out there now, I'm gonna lose this cake job."

"Gonna lose it if you don't go out there. Come on." Roland slipped an arm under Dwight's pits. "You can do twenty minutes with the tadpoles. I have faith."

"Glad one of us does," he muttered.

Dwight's steps were sluggish as they headed to the gate. More than once, Roland had to steer his friend back onto the dirt path. "You okay?"

His response was to start hopping on one foot. "Ow-ow-ow—charley horse!" He bent over, rubbing his calves. "Wooo," he said, straightening up fast, steadying himself with a hand on Roland's shoulder. "Don't wanna do that again. I'm a little d-d-d-dizzy. And my face is killing me."

Roland wondered briefly if he should've paid more attention in first aid class after all. Then he thought, *bang hole,* and decided he didn't care. "C'mon. Skipper's gonna can you if Giggles doesn't show up and do that obnoxious laugh."

"Hee-hoo-ho," Dwight said, but it came out a whimper.

Roland pushed him through the doorway of the fence, then guided the cumbersome giraffe to the back entrance of the small stage in the center of Tiny Town. Each seat on the benches surrounding it was occupied—babies, toddlers, tired-looking parents fanning themselves with park maps as children no older than six stood next to them, waiting to see their favorite characters. "How nice of you to join us!" Hank Hannigan whispered, looking cool and refreshed in his Yaki outfit. Dwight didn't bother to respond; he was wilting, fast, Roland realized. He pointed his friend to face the direction of the audience just as the first bars of the Grilligan's theme song started up.

> *Just sit right back and you'll hear the tale*
> *The tale of a fanciful shrimp*
> *Who jumped upon a hibachi grill*
> *And on teriyaki did not skimp . . .*

Roland did his part, twisting Penny Panda to form the H in shrimp, slapping his knees, hopping about the stage. Dwight was markedly less energetic: his shrimpy R sagged like a limp noodle. As the other costumed characters hooked arms in a clumsy square dance, Giggles the Giraffe stood stage left, long neck tottering precariously forward. That Dwight didn't simply fall flat on his face, scarring the children for life with the visual of Giggles teetering over like a felled tree, was a miracle in itself.

At the end of the song-and-dance number, it was time to spread out among the audience. Parents snapped photos with their iPhones of little Johnny and Jenny sitting on their favorite characters' laps. "Thank god," Dwight mumbled, dropping onto a bench.

A pig-tailed girl of maybe four immediately climbed on his knee, then turned to smile at her dad's camera like she'd been posing for Christmas card shots her whole life. Her little nose wrinkled. "What's that smell?"

The next sound Roland heard was one all Grilligan's employees recognized, and dreaded: the unmistakable *urp*ing of someone trying not to throw up. "Run, kid!" he called out, realizing too late his mistake: the park panda never, ever spoke.

"Penny? You can *talk*?" The wee girl's eyes widened as if witnessing Jesus Christ himself walking on water. The miracle was cut short as a stream of coffee, water, and bile sprayed down Giggles's neck, splattering the little darling's pigtails. An ear-piercing shriek replaced the awe.

"Giggles barfed on me! Daaaaa-dy!" She rocketed off Dwight's lap and threw herself at her father's leg, smearing his pants with vomit. Dad looked a little green around the gills himself. He was peering into the display screen of his fancy-looking Sony Cybershot, and from the grimace he wore, Roland suspected the proud papa had managed to get a shot of his precious daughter right as Giggles spewed on her head.

Dwight seemed oblivious to the commotion, his torso spasming as he continued to dry-heave. A small crowd of boys had formed, bullies circling their prey, and a spiky-haired redhead with freckles dotting every inch of exposed pasty-white skin took the first shot. "Piggles the Giraffe crapped himself! Grossbags!" He winged a paper cup half-full of orange pop at Dwight's back.

The other boys took up the chant. "Pig-gles! Pig-*gles!*"

"Time to go." Roland heaved Dwight to his feet, dragging him away from the benches, through the crowd.

"I think Penny might be a dude," he heard one kid say.

"It's not nice to comment on other people's lifestyle choices," a mother replied.

Roland shoved Dwight through the gate, locking it behind them.

Roland was alarmed to find Dwight's spasming hadn't stopped. *This isn't dry heaving—I think it's a convulsion.* Unable to keep the giraffe upright, he dragged him off the path toward the back john, pulling him about twenty feet into the woods. He ducked under the canopy of an enormous pine, dropping Dwight flat on his back near the trunk. Watching him twitch was unbearable, so Roland ducked under the branches again and pulled off his panda head. He was paralyzed, his thoughts a jumble—what should he do first? Run to the medical station? Dash back to the locker room and find someone to help carry Dwight to safety? Or swipe a cell phone from a park parent and just call 9-1-1?

Why do anything?

Yes, why? The reptile voice had a point.

Now that his one-eyed, convulsing, feces-and-puke-stained buddy was out of sight, Roland had his own problems to think about. He was in big, big trouble if the Skipper caught wind of his rule breach this afternoon. Talking while in Penny uniform. What had he been thinking?

"What *are* you thinking, man? Your buddy is dying here!" Speaking the words aloud stunned Roland back to sanity. The ophidian voice slithered away, retreating into the dark shadows of his mind. He whirled back toward the tree, ducked under, and found the giraffe still at last. *Dead?*—the word struck cold fear in his heart. He stepped closer. *Not dead.* Dwight's chest hitched with shallow, panting breaths. *But soon enough.*

"Dwight? Can you hear me? Just hold tight, buddy. I'm gonna go get help." The medical station was near the Meteor Whirl. Roland could be there in eight minutes, tops, if he jogged, and didn't stop to pose with the kiddies. He gave his friend what he hoped was a reassuring pat on the hoof, and spun to leave. He'd just cleared the pine branches when he heard it—soft, but unmistakable.

It might've been "bring help," the rational Roland voice suggested.

No, it wasn't, the reptile replied.

Roland knew what he'd heard.

Bang hole.

"No, Skipper, I swear. I didn't say a word. You know I wouldn't let you down like that," Roland said. The air conditioning was cranking in the cast director's office, and Roland shivered in spite of himself. He'd made it through two more appearances—even attempting to make a balloon animal for one little boy, though it'd turned out looking more like a squid than a poodle—before getting the dreaded call into the big man's office.

"I don't know what's going on today. Seems like everybody's got a case of the crazies," the rotund man blustered. "I'm getting reports of panda bears talking, giraffes puking—where's your little buddy, by the way? I paged him an hour ago!"

"Who? Dwight?"

"Yeah—you two are tight, right? What the hell's going on with him?"

"I don't know. We're not *that* close, sir. Last I saw—"

The phone on the Skipper's desk cut Roland off. He swallowed down the lie he'd been about to offer.

"Skipper here. What? Are you kidd—what the hell else can go wrong today?" He slammed the phone down in its cradle. Roland held his breath. Had the dying, one-eyed Giggles been discovered already? "We've got another gee-dee turd floating in Wet Dreams. Go on, kid, get out of here—I'm gonna let you off without a written warning this time, but don't let me hear any more nonsense about Penny prattling away with the tykes, got it?" The Skipper waved him away.

Roland nearly bounced back to the cast locker room. Wet Dreams being shut down temporarily meant Allie would have some free time. His next character appearance—the last of the day—wasn't for another thirty minutes. He hoped to make good use of that half hour.

Sure enough, Allie was leaning against the lockers, chatting with a Marilyn. "Hey," she said, turning her sapphire eyes his way when he came in. "Seen Dwight?"

"Uh, Allie . . . can we talk for a minute? Alone, I mean?" Oh, he could get lost in those eyes.

They sat at a bench near the funnel cake booth. Soon her lashes were damp with tears as Roland explained as delicately as possible that her bae wouldn't be calling any time soon. "He's just not that into you," he said, patting her hand.

"I don't understand! Why isn't he telling me this himself?"

"'Cause he's a coward?"

"But last night . . . even this morning, he was all"—she blushed. "Let's just say he insisted on taking a souvenir."

"The panties? I know. He told me all about it."

Now those pretty blue eyes were ice cold. "He what?"

"Allie, I'm sorry. He's just—Dwight's a player. Always has been. And he brags. To everyone. About anyone." *He said you gave the worst head ever*, he almost added, but shook the thought away. If he said it, he'd never get the chance to find out for himself.

A muscle in her jaw flexed, and Roland felt a stirring in his shorts. *How bad could she really be at it?*

"He told you. About my panties."

"Yes." Roland was going to have to play this very carefully, he knew. Be the sympathetic friend, the nice guy, let her cry on his shoulder for the next few weeks, and then, maybe, in an especially vulnerable moment, go in for a kiss, maybe even tongue, if it wasn't too soon . . .

Her eyes narrowed. "What're you doing after work?"

Or maybe things would pick up sooner than he thought.

Dwight had been telling the truth. Allie was a huge letdown. All about *me, me, me,* when really, by the end of the night, he'd just wanted was to get his nut off. Was that too much to ask?

Petulant and needy, and those tan lines hadn't been as alluring as he'd imagined—a thin white strip of skin across her B cups, making them look corpse white against her bronze skin.

Bang hole, Dwight had said. He'd been right.

"Where you going?" she whined as he dressed.

"Home. I live with my parents, and Mom's got a strict curfew." For once, he wasn't embarrassed to admit this sad truth, but rather hoping this would put Allie off. No such luck.

"Call me tomorrow, bae."

Roland's spine stiffened at the order.

He missed Dwight already.

Four police cruisers blocked the Grilligan's entrance the next morning when Roland arrived for his shift. Darn it. He'd been super early, too. After a day as the dreaded panda, he never wanted to miss an opportunity to nab a ninja suit again.

"Hold up there, son." An officer blocked his path.

"What's going on?"

"There's been an incident. We're not letting anyone in yet. Name and identification?"

Roland slid his backpack off his shoulder. He'd carefully cleaned his pocketknife last night, then left it at home. "Roland Girardi. What sort of incident?"

"That's the guy." Roland clenched his teeth at the Skipper's voice. "His little buddy." He was pointing a sausage-like finger in Roland's direction.

Roland blinked and returned his gaze to the policeman in front of him. "What's he talking about? What's going on?"

As the Skipper drew closer, Roland relaxed. His supervisor wore a look of concern and sympathy—not the accusatory outrage he'd imagined at first.

"Skipper? What's all this about?"

Dwight's body had been discovered by Hank Hannigan and one of the Marilyns after park closing, when they'd ducked out back for a little snogging under the stars. "It was the smell," the Skipper said in a reverential whisper. "You know how hot it was yesterday. Meat tends to spoil pretty fast in heat like that." A look of self-disgust crossed his face. "I can't believe I just said that. Sorry, kid."

"We're all upset," Roland said, feeling grown up. The reptile voice had grown claws and feet, taking control, and so far, he'd commanded the ship called Roland into appropriately grieved and puzzled reactions. "Don't beat yourself up about it. I just can't believe I didn't realize—when he was puking, you know, I shoulda figured heat stroke . . ."

"Kid was a partier," the Skipper said with an empathetic clap on the shoulder. "Showed up hungover every day. How could you have known? You can't blame yourself for this."

Roland knew this wasn't so, that he was one hundred percent to blame. But he didn't argue with the big man. *Smooth sailing ahead, Captain!* the reptile proclaimed.

Grilligan's was closed most of the morning, though open and running in time for the lunchtime crowd. The police had cleared the scene in the back woods, and had set up camp in the Skipper's office to question the staff. By then, whispers of something decidedly darker than heat stroke were making their way through the employee grapevine.

"Someone cut his eye out," the less-pretty Marilyn told Roland solemnly after the one o'clock show. "You have to really hate someone to do that, you know?"

"So they think it was someone who knew him?"

"Yeah. Someone with an axe to grind."

"Huh."

"What? What do you know?" The Marilyn leaned in conspiratorially, but Roland shook his head.

"Nothing. I shouldn't talk out of school." He suppressed a grin at her questioning gaze, the one that said *yes, you absolutely must.* "It's just that he and Allie hooked up the other night and—well, let's just say it meant more to her than him, and she wasn't happy about it. At all."

"Roland? Baby? Is it true?"

Allie's harping voice made Roland shudder. He ignored her, whispering quickly. "But cutting an eye out? Sure, she was pretty mad, but it doesn't make any sense—they search everyone—all of us, staff and guests, for weapons before we can even get in. What about the metal detectors?"

"Oh, come on now," Marilyn scoffed. "Half the time the security people aren't even here yet when we come in. Besides, you can make a weapon of anything. I once had a little jerk of a kid stab me with a cotton candy cone so hard it drew blood."

"*There* you are," Allie said. She hooked a possessive arm through Roland's, glaring at the Marilyn. "I just heard the news. What happened, do you think?"

She cocked her pretty head up at Roland, tilting it just so, and batted her lashes. Roland leaned back slightly, eyeballing her bun—yup, there it was—then locking Marilyn in a knowing stare. The platinum blonde's eyes widened as the sun glittered off the sparkles of the sheet metal starfish.

"Excuse me. I think I hear the Skipper calling me," Marilyn stammered. She hurried off in the direction of the cast director's office.

"Are you okay? I just can't believe it—Dwight." She let out a dramatic half-sob. "Out there in the woods, all alone. Oh!" She blanched. "You don't think—was he still wearing my . . . that won't get me in trouble, will it?"

"I'm sure you have nothing to worry about," Roland assured her, his words serpentine.

MISS ELIZABETH'S POISON

The murders, I fear, were ultimately my fault. I just didn't believe she really had it in her.

I've never misjudged anyone so horrendously.

Let me explain. My name is Gussie Gilchrist, and I work for my father in the local apothecary shop here in Fall River. My job is to sweep the floors and dust the glass globes filled with colored water that shimmer in the front window. I polish our wooden counters, clean the windows that are always propped open during this hot, steamy August, and shoo out the wayward insects that find their way in to buzz among our scented soaps and imported chocolates.

However, these are not my only tasks. Father and I share a secret. He is now practically blind, and it is I who mixes the potions, crushes the herbs with mortar and pestle in the back room, and fills the orders. If any of his customers knew it was a mere girl mixing their tonics and salves, he'd be ruined. So I act the part of shopkeeper's assistant, wiping down the cigar case and making sure the match dispenser is filled. When a customer comes in with an ailment, Father calls out to me to make sure the measuring glasses and pill-rolling machine are cleaned and ready, and I hurry off to the back room to prepare the medicine.

I am a quick study. At seventeen, I already know which plants and mineral salts are best for which ailments. We use a mixture of sodium phosphate and citric acid to cure constipation, and heroin mixed with cherry syrup to sedate coughs. For a bad cold, ten grains of opium do the trick, and nothing restores health and vitality like a dose of French tonic wine. We carry effervescent salts for headaches and seasickness, and when our customers are wracked with pain for which the only end will be death, that's when we dispense the morphine. My potions are second to none. But 'tis the scared women, who come in right before closing, when father has already retired for the evening leaving me to clean up, that are my best customers.

I can recognize them right away. They duck into our doorway with wide eyes and trembling shoulders, like they're ready to jump out of their own skin. They're all frightened, desperate, and ready to try anything. It's my job to assess the situation and decide if they're really capable of executing the solution they've sought me out to find.

The ones who have found themselves in a family way are the easiest to figure out. Most of them are unmarried, the victim of a cruel attack, perverse family member, or the simple promise of true love and a marriage proposal that never came. These ladies cry on my shoulder, afraid to tell their parents or pastor of their terrible woe, but so scared and fraught, they're willing to spill all to me, a stranger. Perhaps because I'm a woman, they think I'll understand. I can't imagine the stark hopelessness and terror some of these poor girls felt when they were taken against their will, oftentimes by men they trusted. When their cheeks are ruddy and they can no longer speak for sobbing, this is when I decide if they truly need my help.

For most of these ladies, I hand them a potion of bitter melon, nutmeg, and wild carrot to induce miscarriage. Father taught me this potion only once, after a young girl of twelve found herself in an awful way after being assaulted by a stranger, but I have a memory for such things. Yet once in a while, a young woman will show up, newly married and simply afraid of motherhood, and I refuse to help such twits. When this type of girl arrives, asking for assistance simply because she's worried that she won't be a suitable mother, I prepare a mixture of lime and coconut juice, and when it does nothing but give them mild gas, I assure them that it is merely God's will that she have the baby after all. So you see, I am not blind to the power I hold. I need to choose wisely when it comes to the women I help.

This is especially true of the ladies that come in for darker purposes. Some wish to escape an unhappy marriage; others simply want to end their own miserable existences. These are the gray women, slinking through the door shrouded in dark coats, chin down, uneasily determined to end a life. I have to study these ladies closely, listen to their tales, wipe away their tears, and decide if I can, in fact, provide them with the end result they seek. Some of these women have husbands who beat them mercilessly for the most ridiculous of imagined slights— Prudence Cooper, for instance, showed me her permanently disfigured hands, each finger broken after her husband caught her penning a thank-you note to her sister for sending over a basket of berries.

"He's never liked Esther, you see," Prudence said, wincing at the memory. "Thinks she's uppity because she married a banker. It was my fault; I know he doesn't want me to have contact with her, but those strawberries were the best I'd ever tasted. Plus, she's my *sister*. I couldn't just—I had to—and this?" She held up her bent claws, healed in a mishmash of angles, and set her shoulders back. "I can't take it anymore. How can anyone live like this?"

If I think they really do have it in them, the capacity for murder, and the man whose life they're hoping to end seems to truly deserve it, I might wrap up a neat bottle of prussic acid in simple brown paper, tie it tight with twine, and send them off to their dark deed. Of these women, of which I've helped no more than eight, none have been suspected of murder. And why would they be? On the rare occasion that the local constable stops by to ask if Mrs. Cooper or Mrs. Bell might have come in, inquiring about poison to rid oneself of mice, my father confidently assures them that this never happened.

When Miss Elizabeth came in that night, shaking out her black umbrella and wiping her boots neatly on the doormat, I was surprised. Her father is notoriously tight with his pennies, and we rarely see his daughters in here to look over our boxed candy or fancy bottles of perfume. I recognized her, of course, from church. How many times had I seen her drab figure, her ashy blonde curls with tendrils of wiry gray sneaking through, and thought *there, but for the grace of God* . . . ? No, I did not envy Miss Elizabeth, for under her demeanor, her proud jaw and thin lips, was always an air of strain: she was wound tighter than piano wire, and every sharp movement and short reply she gave made one think she would snap at any moment under the tension of her life. I suppose I shouldn't have been surprised that she'd found her way to me, to seek out a potion to ease her burden. But you see, I never thought she had it in her.

I stood for a moment, broom in hand, staring at her as she brushed the droplets off her overcoat. She lifted her head up and walked directly toward me, with purpose.

"We're closed," I offered weakly, but she shook her head, and came close enough to make me uncomfortable.

"I'm not here for a bottle of nerve tonic," she said, then smiled tightly. "I need a special sort of medicine this evening, and I'm told you're the only one who might be able to supply such a thing." I blinked. Heard from whom? Perhaps I should concern myself more with what gossips were saying on the street?

"I'm sure I don't know what you mean," I replied, more confident than I felt. Was it Prudence Cooper who betrayed my secret? I should never have trusted that nervous little mouse. I should slip a little something into *her* nerve tonic . . . though now that her husband William had met his maker, she rarely had need of our wares. I reluctantly met Miss Elizabeth's eyes and shook my head slightly. "What was it you were looking for?"

"Oh, calm down, Gussie. You're shaking like a frightened child. I need something special, that's all. A bit of an unusual request. Surely you can help me?"

"What did you have in mind?" I asked, leaning my broom against the counter by the soap display. I had to proceed cautiously, in case Miss Elizabeth was trying to trap me. I wouldn't put it past her to try and earn a few pennies as a police informant if the opportunity arose.

"A bottle of prussic acid, if you would." My eyes grew wide, but she held up a gloved hand before I could protest. "Just to clean a sealskin cloak. That's all," she said, and her tight smile returned. I didn't trust that smile. I didn't trust the black look in her eyes, or the squint to her cheeks that made her face look constricted. No, something wasn't right here at all.

"I don't know that we have that in stock," I said, hoping she would accept my lie and leave. "Father doesn't like to keep much of that around, in case of robbery. It can be quite toxic, you know." I looked at her again, and the shadow in her eyes told me that she did know how toxic the acid was; knew well, indeed, for what she was asking. "What matter of stain are you trying to get out? Perhaps we have some sort of oil or polish that could help."

"I've scrubbed it with a bit of ash and water, to no avail," she replied. "Really, I've tried everything. My girl Maggie soaked it for a whole day, but the spot just won't come out. Surely you have something," she added. "I'm afraid the cloak in question isn't wearing well, and it's also starting to look shabby. I was told that prussic acid would refresh it quite nicely. Nothing else will do, you understand."

Oh, I understood. If she needed the prussic acid to clean a sealskin cloak, one of the finest furs on the market that could hold up to the worst weather New England had to offer with nary a bald patch, then I was a monkey's uncle. No, her intent with the poison was for a darker purpose, I was sure. But who? She was unmarried, and had no prospects for a beau that I'd heard; her sister Emma was considered the attractive one in the family, and even she had not stepped out with a gentleman for a good number of years. Was Miss Elizabeth jealous of her older sister's beauty? Yet the two seemed close . . . perhaps it was her father, who had made a fortune buying and selling textile mills, yet had not seen it fit to upgrade his house with indoor plumbing or an icebox. Or maybe her stepmother, Abby Gray, was the intended target. Though Miss Elizabeth had never publicly spoken ill against the woman who had married Mister Andrew when Miss Elizabeth was but five, I had noticed that Miss Elizabeth and Miss Emma often sat a bit apart from Mister Andrew and Mrs. Abby at Sunday services.

Any one of this cast of characters could be in trouble, I realized. Usually, when a lady comes to me in a desperate hope to solve her troubles, they spill out their tale in a flurry of tears and torment. I decided to press her further.

"Miss Elizabeth, unfortunately, I can't just dispense prussic acid at the drop of a coin. If you could tell me a little more about your situation, your true intent . . ."

Her eyebrows arched, then furrowed angrily. Miss Elizabeth was having none of my prying. She wanted prussic acid to clean a coat, and no further discussion was to take place. I studied her face for a moment, her clenched jaw ticking, and nodded. She was not going to leave until she got what she wanted.

If she wasn't going to be honest with me, I saw no need to be honest with her. I brushed past her to the back room and pulled out my glass measuring tubes. I would give her a potion, all right: a poison to upset the stomach, no more, and if she were so determined to do away with someone, she would have presented herself in much more of a distressed fashion. She was toying with me; for what purpose, I did not know, but I was not about to give her the satisfaction of finding out my own dark secret, my ability to dole out death where death was due. The bottle I wrapped up would not only cause stomach cramps, but in a pinch, would do a fine job of cleaning a wayward spot on a sealskin cloak. She could have that. No more.

She paid me with four cold copper coins and a nod, and left quickly, without a word. I locked the door behind her, and hurried home to serve Father his stew. Potatoes and a bit of ham tonight; he'd be pleased.

Imagine my shock when I saw the headlines today! That Miss Elizabeth has been accused of doing away with both her father and stepmother with an axe! What behavior, what incident, could have put her in such a rage, the papers speculated? What madness lay beneath this proper, proud woman, to incite her to do such a deed? But I know. I know exactly why she was so enraged, and who, exactly, is to blame.

Yes, I am sure that Miss Elizabeth had been angry enough to hack away at both her father and stepmother until they bled to death, their features unrecognizable. She must have administered the poison, and watched, and waited; perhaps when her family complained of stomach upset, her hopes rose. It was working. The poison was taking effect, and soon her problems would be over. How frustrated she must have been when she saw them suffer, but not die; as the realization dawned on her that she was nursing these awful people through their sweats and aches, for naught. They would recover.

Yes, she must have been furious. With me.

As fortune would have it, our apothecary was closed yesterday, so I could accompany Father to the countryside to obtain some colt's foot to combat the bout of bronchial congestion that had taken hold of half the town. Summer pneumonia is not to be trifled with, and demand for this herb has been high. Father and I drove out of town to a particularly rich field we often visit, and so our shop windows were dark when Miss Elizabeth stopped by for a second time with murder on her mind.

After I read the news, I confessed Miss Elizabeth's visit to Father. I left out the details of the other women I've helped, but I told him of her desire to purchase prussic acid, and admitted that I'd sold her a solution of aloe vera mixed with saline. I told him that it seemed peculiar, the way she came in as I was closing, as if she was carrying out some murky deed. I asked him, wide-eyed, if we should inform the constable. Father agreed immediately, and congratulated me on my honesty, and my refusal to give her the poison. If he only knew!

I will admit my intentions are not particularly noble. Miss Elizabeth has clearly shown the extent of her rage and fury. I must do my part to put her behind bars.

I can well imagine on whom her black eyes will turn next if she is acquitted.

EAT YOUR VEGETABLES

"I'm off to my meeting," Annie called out.

"Meeting?" Doug was planted in the La-Z-Boy, watching reruns of *NCIS*.

"Remember, I told you I was joining Weight Watchers? They meet on Thursdays at the senior center. Tonight's my first weigh-in."

"You look beautiful," Doug said as she pulled the front door shut behind her.

Annie didn't *feel* beautiful. She felt like a waddling, middle-aged blob with bad knees and no chin. At her last physical, her doctor had announced that her body mass index now officially put her in the "obese" category. That was six months ago, and she'd *tried* to be good. Had salads for lunch for almost a week. But then someone's granddaughter was selling Girl Scout cookies, and shamrock shakes were back at McDonalds . . .

Spring was just around the corner, and bathing suit season would be here soon. She'd caught herself practically wheezing at work when she'd had to lug the donated books to the library basement. She was only fifty-one. Enough was enough. She needed to lose weight.

And Doug was one to talk. In the twenty-five years they'd been married, he'd put on his fair share of weight, too. He liked to joke that he was always ready for the beach—"got the beach ball packed and ready to go," he'd say, patting his belly. Had she laughed at that? Probably. His growing girth had made it more acceptable that she'd been putting on pounds, too.

She drove the ten miles with butterflies in her stomach. She was afraid of how far the needle would climb when she stepped on the scale. Of what the woman weighing her in would say. Annie hoped the woman wasn't perky. She didn't think she could deal with perky tonight.

"Great news: you're at 181. That's a great place to launch from!" the perky weigh-in woman announced. Annie wanted to punch her in the face.

"How so? I'm fatter than an entire kindergarten class. That's twelve five-year-olds, with one to spare."

"Aren't you funny? Just think—you're only a pound away from a lower decade! Seventies, here we come!"

Perkalicious had a point. It would be a nice ego boost to see the 170s again.

Annie scooped up her coat and an armful of materials—recipes, directions on how to download and sign in to the Weight Watchers app, a free sample of two-point brownie bites. In the room, people had begun to arrive and take seats.

Annie sat on an uncomfortable gray folding chair and waited for the meeting to start.

"First time?" A rotund woman with long black hair and Harry Potter glasses settled in next to her.

"First time in years. How'd you know?"

"You look terrified. Most people talk a friend into going. You don't have any fat friends?"

Annie let out a nervous laugh.

"Well, now you do. Name's Dee." She held out a hand, and Annie took it gratefully. "I've been doing the program for three months now. Down fifteen pounds. It's slow, but it works. Slower after menopause, but what the hell. If Oprah's willing to stick it out, so am I." A thin woman with curly chestnut hair moved to the front of the room, waving her hands. Dee eyeballed her and kept talking. "If you need tips on low-point sugary snacks, I'm your gal. I can calculate the points value of *anything*, on sight. Here's Erica, our group leader. She's so bubbly I want to stick her in a soda bottle and shake her up 'til she pops, but she's motivating, I'll give her that."

Annie smiled. It felt good to make a new friend.

After congratulating all the audience members who'd hit milestones (including one man who'd hit the 100-pound loss mark—"men always lose faster, the lucky turds," Dee whispered), Erica recapped *her* story. She'd lost seventy-six pounds of "baby weight" on Weight Watchers after her third child was born, and had kept it off for six years. Tonight's motivational speech was on incorporating exercise into everyday activities. "You can do aerobics while folding clothes," Erica enthused, miming a ridiculous bend-and-stretch with an imaginary towel. "And gardening is a *great* activity! It's seed-planting time, people, and when you do all that hard work of tilling and planting and weeding, your garden will reward you with a bounty of zero-point foods! See? It's win-win!"

"Except for corn," someone piped up from behind Annie and Dee. "Corn costs points."

"Killjoy," Dee hissed, but Annie wasn't paying attention. Erica was right. When they were newlyweds, Doug and Annie had put a vegetable garden in the back, just past the shed, for a couple of years. She had fond memories of picking snap peas with her mother, and had wanted to continue the tradition. But they'd had no kids of their own for her to share the experience with, and maintaining it *was* hard work. They'd let the garden fall by the wayside, and over the years, the weeds had taken over as the rototiller sat rusting in the shed. But she'd enjoyed gardening. Hadn't she?

She exchanged phone numbers with Dee and left the meeting full of hope and energy. She could *do* this plan. She was ready to commit. And this weekend, she was going to hit Mackey's for supplies and get her garden in.

"Are you kidding? $16.99 for this little box of MiracleGro? Are we fertilizing with gold?" Doug's voice carried over the aisles of the garden center.

"Shut up, Doug. It'll make me happy. You *do* want to make me happy, right?"

"I've been eating fish and broccoli for three days, woman! Your Weight Watchers cult meetings have upended my whole routine. You tossed my Cheetos and swapped out my Wonder Bread for that flat pita crap. Isn't that enough for you?" Doug put the box of MiracleGro back on the shelf. "This is where I draw the line. I'm sure our seeds will grow just fine with plain old dirt and water."

Annie pouted. If she was going to put in the effort—she'd put up stakes and deer netting that very morning while Doug had worked on cleaning up the rototiller and getting it running, and yes, it *had* been an effort—she wanted to do it right. But her stomach was squeezing uncomfortably, still adjusting to the influx of fiber in her diet, and she didn't have time to argue. She needed a bathroom.

"Fine. You take this up front and pay," she said, handing Doug her seed packets, gardening gloves, and trowel. "I need the ladies' room." She hurried off to the back corner where she'd seen a sign.

After her potty break (*every moment on the bowl is one step closer to your goal,* Dee had texted just yesterday), Annie nearly ran into a stooped brown man with a freckled scalp waiting for the restroom. "I'm so sorry," she said, stepping aside.

The old man held up a tanned, wrinkled hand. It was thick and calloused, and resembled nothing so much as a bear's paw. "No need to apologize, my dear. I was actually waiting for you."

"Well, it's all yours." Annie waved a hand at the bathroom.

"No, no. I heard you earlier. Starting a garden? Heard your husband say something about Weight Watchers. Going to meetings or doing it online?"

"Meetings," Annie murmured. She took a small step back. Why was this old man so interested in her diet? "Excuse me— my husband's waiting for me." She tried to step to the side, but he mirrored her movement, continuing to block her path.

"Great idea, growing your own vegetables. Your husband's right, you know. The price of fertilizer is outrageous these days.

That's why I make my own." He broke out in a wide grin. Several teeth were missing, and one in the front was twisted like a piece of ribbon candy. Annie flinched before she could stop herself.

The bronzed old man seemed not to notice. "Old family recipe. Make it all year, then sell it in the spring to supplement the income. You know. Cash only and all that. Uncle Sam takes enough as it is. You wouldn't tell on a grizzled old farmer, would you?"

Annie shook her head. She didn't care if he made a few bucks under the table. Hell, she'd be retiring herself a few years down the road, and would probably do the same, if she could think of something clever enough to sell. "Fertilizer, you say? Does it work on vegetables?"

"Like a charm," he said, and wheezed out a laugh. "Got some in my truck. Why don't you and your hubby follow me over to the Burger King parking lot, and maybe we can do a little business?" Annie nodded. The man seemed harmless enough, and he'd suggested a public place. What harm could it do?

Annie bought three bags of Farmer Paul's Fantastical Fertilizer from the old man while Doug went inside for a Whopper.

"Really? You're going to make me do all the heavy lifting?" she shouted to her husband as he hustled inside.

"You're trying to starve me to death!" he threw back. Annie grumbled, and turned back to the farmer. He had two bags hefted onto his shoulder.

"Want them in the back?"

Annie scrambled to pop the trunk of her Camry. The old farmer slid the bags smoothly from his shoulder into the trunk.

He tugged a third bag from the bed of his pickup and carried it over, plopping it on top of the other two with a *thunk*.

"Pleasure doing business with you," he said. "You local?"

"Yes, we're in town," Annie replied. "You?"

"In town, for now. I'm what you'd call a migrant worker, I suppose. Follow the planting season across the country, getting work where I can. Bit of a gypsy, you might say. Right now, I'm working at the Ellis farm near the Gilead Hill Cemetery. You know it?" Annie nodded. "Come on by the farm if you need more." He offered his twisted grin once more, and Annie beamed back at him.

"Three bags for ten dollars," she said to Doug on the drive home. "What a deal!"

"Better than MiracleGro," Doug agreed. "Better work."

"You've lost two-point-three pounds! Isn't that wonderful?" Perkalicious announced at Annie's weigh-in.

"That's it? I thought most people had a big loss the first week." Annie scowled.

"Everyone's different. Come on. You're 178.7 now. Welcome to the seventies!"

Annie offered a half-hearted smile and collected her things. She found Dee sitting next to a young woman with maybe twenty pounds to lose. She had short red hair, and a large tattoo of a blue butterfly spanning the back of her neck. Annie wondered if she kept her hair so short just to show off that little bit of artwork.

"You gonna eat that brownie?" Annie heard Dee ask. "Oh, here you are, Annie. This is Katrina. How'd you do?"

Annie reported her first week's results.

"Menopause," Dee said knowingly.

By the end of the week, Annie had everything planted. She'd done a little at a time after work each day, until the tomatoes, radishes, cucumbers, green beans, and spaghetti squash were all sown in neat rows. On Saturday, she spread the fertilizer.

"Smells like holy hell," Doug said from his perch on the riding mower.

It *did* smell awful. Like cat urine and raisins and decay. "I don't care what it smells like, as long as it works," she shot back. But she stopped to go back inside and put on long sleeves and gloves. She didn't want the stink to cling to her.

At next week's meeting, she was down another pound. "That's great news," said Dee, who was also down.

"I lost four and a half pounds!" Katrina said, beaming as she took her seat.

"Let's kill her and barbeque her for dinner," Annie muttered. "I'm freakin' starving."

The radishes were the first to come in, and they were unlike any radishes Annie had ever seen. She was weeding carefully, her knees barking in pain, when she noticed the phosphorescent blue bulbs pushing up from the soil, like sapphires in the sun. She tugged one out from the earth and wiped off the dirt with one gloved hand.

The radish was squat and plump, almost perfect in its uniform smoothness. It was fatter than any radish she'd seen at the local farmer's market. It was the blue root head—shimmering and layered, like an otherworldly star—that mesmerized her. She stared at it for a moment, then twisted off the spidery tip and bit down.

A sharp, peppery burst of flavor filled her mouth. She crunched, her teeth grinding on the dirt that still clung to the skin, and smiled. She closed her eyes, letting the sun dry her sweat-dampened skin, and as she rolled the radish chunks across her tongue, she thought of her mother. Of warm spring afternoons when her mom would tug at the quackgrass and pigweed while young Annie followed behind, picking hornworms off of the tomatoes and squishing them between her chubby fingers. Of her mother's floppy yellow gardening hat and dirt-smeared overalls. Of the earthy taste of green beans, snapped fresh off the plant.

Annie opened her eyes. Radish tops surrounded her like tiny salad corpses. She'd eaten half the row without even thinking about it.

Her cheeks flushed as she pulled up the rest of the vegetables. *No need to tell Doug*, and then: *So what if you do? They're zero points.* She popped another blue radish in her mouth and took a fistful into the house.

"We have radishes!" she called out, slipping out of her Crocs.

"Already? How fast do those things grow?" Doug's voice came from above. Annie brushed off her butt and legs, then climbed the stairs from basement to kitchen.

"Pretty fast, I guess. I don't think the seeds in the packet were the same type of radish as the picture on the cover," she said. "Look at these things."

"Good job, hon. They look like giant alien blueberries. Are they *supposed* to be blue?"

"I guess so. I didn't look at what kind of radishes they were when we bought the seeds."

"Huh. Must be some exotic strain. From Mexico or something."

"Because the radishes grow blue in Mexico?" she asked with a laugh. "Want some? I was going to chop them up and make a salad."

"No, thanks. I hate radishes."

"177.7," Perkalicious said. "Exactly where you were last week. Good news: you didn't gain!"

"But I didn't lose, either. How can that be? I ate steamed broccoli as a *snack*. Surely there's some payoff for my suffering?"

"Maybe you're hitting a plateau," Perkalicious said.

"Aren't I a little early in the process to be plateauing? Erica says that usually happens in the third month."

Perkalicious shrugged. "Everyone's different."

Annie stormed to her seat and practically threw her extra vegetables at Dee and Katrina. "Here. I have radishes coming out my ears."

"Thanks," Katrina said. Dee made a face, and handed her bouquet to the redhead. "Double for you. Radishes give me heartburn. Why are they blue?"

"They're Mexican radishes," Annie said with a shrug.

Erica's motivational speech that night was about changing one's mindset. "It's not all or nothing, gang," she effervesced. "One slip does not a diet ruin. Use your flex points, earn some activity points, and get right back on the horse."

I'd feel more motivated if I'd actually slipped, Annie fumed.

Doug was waiting for her when she got home. "How was your meeting? Guess what?" he added, before she could answer. "I'm down eleven pounds! I don't even know how I did it!"

"*I* did it for you, you dumbbell!" Annie exploded. "*I* cook all the dinners. *I* do all the grocery shopping. You've lost weight because *I'm* on a diet."

"Hey, now, don't I get some credit? I did carry the laundry upstairs last week. Twice. That's *exercise*," he said with a self-satisfied grin.

It was hard for Annie not to chuckle. "I hate you," she said, but there was love behind the words.

The cucumber vines were spreading like tentacles. "I'm worried they'll choke out the tomatoes," Annie told Doug, surveying the garden with her fists on her hips.

"The garden really looks great, hon. Are those green beans I see?"

Annie squinted at the rows of leafy plants in the back corner of the garden. Doug was right: there were thin, twisted fingers of beans peeking out from beneath the leaves.

"How can that be? I'm *sure* they take two months. My mom would plant the garden the first weekend in May, and we'd pick green beans on the fourth of July. What kind of beans did we plant?"

"Maybe it's the fertilizer. I'll go get you something to put the beans in." Doug shuffled back toward the house as Annie carefully made her way to the ripening plants, stepping cautiously around the cucumber vines. She squatted to look closer.

They were dark green, almost emerald, and she could see the outline of the beans within the pod through the gossamer skin. They weren't straight like the pole beans of her youth: they curled grotesquely, like worms caught in the sun after a heavy rain. She plucked one off the plant and snapped it in half. *They smell like summer*, she decided, and ate it. It tasted sweet and tender and sunbaked. She picked another, and then a handful more; by the time Doug came back with a black garbage bag ("best thing I could find") she'd stripped two plants clean.

It took an hour for Annie to pick all the beans. Her garbage bag was filled to overflowing, and Doug had to carry it back to the house for her. She scrubbed and cleaned six colanders' worth, trimming the stems and carefully parceling out the beans into freezer bags. After she had ten bags packaged, and another strainer's full to steam for dinner, she gave up. The rest of the still-stuffed bag could go to the girls at Weight Watchers.

Annie's stomach started gurgling as she steamed the beans and grilled the tilapia for dinner. She and Doug watched a re-run of *Six Feet Under* as they ate. She shifted uncomfortably on the couch as she forked down her fish; her pants suddenly felt too tight. She put down her plate. *Too many green beans,* she thought. *There's a good ounce of fish still left on my plate. Gotta remember to give myself a point back for that.*

As the evening wore on, she and Doug found themselves tag-teaming their way in and out of the bathroom. It had to be the beans.

"Guess we're getting older," Doug said, letting loose a noisy burst of gas. "System can't handle all that fiber anymore." Sighing, Annie tossed her carefully prepared freezer bags on top of the other beans in the garbage bag. So much for home farming.

"180. Don't get discouraged; this happens," Perkalicious said, but she wasn't making eye contact. "Maybe you could change things up. Drink more water, increase your vegetable intake, that kind of thing."

"*Increase* my vegetable intake? Are you kidding? I made a lasagna constructed completely out of green beans this week!"

"Ooh, I love fresh green beans."

"Well, there's a ten-pound garbage bag full of 'em on the registration table right now. Help yourself." Annie snatched her weigh-in card from the girl and stalked to her seat.

"I'm up," she snapped.

"Yeah, I guessed," Dee said. She leaned over and dropped her voice to a whisper. "If it makes you feel any better, Katrina's up four pounds. In one week! The weigh-in girl asked her if she was tracking *all* her points. Kat said she wanted to smack her in the face with a box of brownie bi—" Dee stopped abruptly as Katrina took the seat to Annie's left.

"Green beans," Katrina said. "Zero points, fuckers." She started cramming the vegetables in her mouth, gnashing furiously.

Annie turned back to Dee, eyebrows raised. "By the way, I brought in some more veggies from the garden. They're at the check-in table. Help yourself."

"Thanks, but I'm good," Dee said, and settled back as Erica started her lecture.

There were cucumbers everywhere. They'd taken over the garden.

Annie gawked at the snarl of black vines choking out the other plants. Thick tendrils curled up the tomato stalks, ending in long, prickered fruits that looked positively obscene among the pale green tomatoes. Annie hurried back into the house.

"Doug? I'm going to need help with these cucumbers!"

The two of them worked silently, side by side, occasionally holding up a particularly large specimen for the other to see. They filled two garbage bags, then a third. "How many seeds did you *plant*?" Doug grumbled at one point. Annie was sure it had been only twelve: three seeds, four hills. She'd already gone over the planting process in her head several times, seeking out and re-tabulating the small hills from which the gnarled, creeping briars sprang forth.

"I've never seen anything like this," Annie said with a sigh. "Maybe you were right—maybe it was that fertilizer?"

"That guy could make a fortune selling it to third-world countries," Doug said. "This is crazy."

As dusk settled in across the backyard, Annie and Doug hauled their bounty indoors. "I'll put out a box tomorrow by the road."

"Like a farm stand?" Annie asked.

"Like a 'take our free vegetables, *please*' stand."

Annie nodded. "I'll do what I can tonight—I saw a recipe for freezer pickles online that I want to try—but yeah, I think giving them away by the road sounds fine. Even if everyone at my meeting takes three each, we'd still have a ton left."

Annie chopped up cucumbers and tossed them with fat-free Italian dressing, and she and Doug had them with dinner. They were crisp and sweet—by far the best cukes she'd ever tasted. *Finally, a vegetable I can eat with abandon.* She and Doug finished off the first bowl of cucumber salad, and she made more for the rest of the week. Then she toiled late into the night, slicing and freezing.

After work the next afternoon, Annie pulled on her gardening gloves and went out to see if she could release the chokehold the cucumber vines had on the tomato plants. She screamed when she got to the garden fence.

The cucumbers had multiplied overnight.

They were an alien, horticultural hydra: for every cucumber she and Doug had picked yesterday, two now poked out in their place. Smaller than the ones they'd harvested, sure, but there were green cylinders *everywhere*. She couldn't even see the underripe tomatoes any more.

She heard Doug panting behind her. "Are you okay? What's wrong?" He grabbed her arm, spun her toward him, and gave her a once-over. "You screamed. Are you bleeding?"

She shook her head. "Look!" was all she managed, pointing to the garden.

"Ho-*lee* hell." Doug whistled.

"That's it. I quit. I can't keep up with—with—" she gestured again at the snarled mess. "*This!*"

"Are you sure you want to give up now? It's good exercise, and honestly, maybe that'll help."

"*What?*"

"I don't mean anything by it. You're beautiful just as you are. But you've been working so hard at your diet, and it's just lately—well, I hate to see you give up after all that effort. Forget it. Forget I said anything."

"Oh, keep talking, fat boy," she said, her eyes narrowing.

"Hey, now. Don't be mean."

"I'm not the only one putting on weight, pal. You were so proud over the weight you dropped a couple of weeks ago, but if we're being honest here, you've put it right back on, and then some. Guess what, kettle? You're black." Annie started to cry. "I can't believe you called me fat!"

Doug wrapped his arms around her. She pretended not to notice that his hands barely met at her back. "You're gorgeous just as you are," he said. "More of you to love."

"I hate you," she said. But she didn't mean it.

Annie passed out bags of cucumbers at the next meeting like goodie bags at a party. Katrina bit into the end of one like a hungry dog attacking fresh meat.

"Everything okay?" Annie asked, studying the woman. She looked . . . bloated.

"Sure. Okay, no. I'm up another six pounds this week. Everyone is. It doesn't make sense."

"I feel your pain," Annie said with a sigh. "I'm up three."

"I'm down a half a pound," Dee announced with a wide smile.

Katrina turned on her, eyes blazing. "How are you *doing* that? Annie's been bringing in fresh veggies every week, and you haven't taken even one radish. I never hear you sharing recipes or talking about non-fat sour cream. What's your secret?"

Dee grinned sheepishly. "I stay within my points, simple as that. If I choose to spend all my points on Tootsie Roll midgees, well, I do that. I don't *like* vegetables. I like sweets."

Annie rolled her eyes. "I like my sweets, too. But if I didn't supplement my food intake with points-free food, I'd be starving all the time. Six midgees for four points aren't going to sustain me."

Dee opened her mouth to respond, but Erica cut her off from the front of the room. The meeting leader's smile looked forced, and Annie had a flash of memory: Heath Ledger as the Joker, asking partygoers if they knew *why* he always smiled. She couldn't remember the answer.

"We're going to have a change of topic this week. I was going to talk about positive internal dialogue, but I've had a few requests that we discuss overcoming a setback. Seems like we've had quite a few slips this week."

Annie studied Erica. Did she look a little . . . rounder around the edges? And pale—sickly, almost. Annie stole a glance at Katrina next to her. Same pasty skin. Was something going around?

"Erica's dead," Dee announced when Annie answered her phone the next morning. "Collapsed on her treadmill. The rumor is heart attack."

"How on earth? She couldn't have been that old." Annie put down the cucumber slice she'd speared with her fork. "So she worked and sweated her butt off to lose over seventy-five pounds, only to drop dead on the treadmill? And leave three kids? Kinda makes you wonder if . . . well, if it's even worth it." Her mind wandered to the Girl Scouts that had been sitting outside of the grocery store just the other day, table loaded with Thin Mints. *Should've grabbed a box. Life is short.*

"I know. It doesn't make sense. Erica was the healthiest, most gung-ho Weight Watcher I've ever met, and I've been on and off this plan my whole life. I don't get it."

"Maybe she had high cholesterol or something."

"Maybe."

"Listen, Dee . . . I'm thinking about quitting the plan. It's just—it's not working for me. I've been more careful with my points than Ebenezer Scrooge was with his gold. I've taxed my creativity trying to come up with tasty ways to eat vegetables. I tried making cucumber fries the other night. They tasted like saltwater mush. I—I think I need to try something else. A different diet, maybe."

"Give it one more meeting," Dee said. "I'll help you. We can walk the track at the high school a couple times this week. I have a bottle of Liquid Smoke that'll make your cucumbers taste like barbecued ribs, no points added. Don't give up yet. Besides, aren't you curious to see what'll happen this week? Now that our fearless leader is no more?"

Annie could feel her cheeks stretch with her smile. "You're right. Thanks, Dee. I needed a cheerleader."

She met Dee at the track on Monday and Wednesday. Thursday afternoon, she was feeling hopeful as she squeezed her eyes shut and stepped on Perkalicious's scale.

"Oh. My."

Annie's eyes flew open. She looked at the numbers in front of her.

190.5. She'd gained seven and a half pounds. In one week. After adding more exercise and not using a single flex point. "I quit," Annie said.

Perkalicious inhaled, looking like she was gearing up to argue, but she seemed to be struggling to find the words. Annie kept on talking before the woman could convince her to give it more time. "I've *gained* almost ten pounds since I started this plan. I'm tracking *every point* that goes into my mouth. I'm using lettuce for bread and cucumber slices for meat in my sandwiches. I'm doing everything right. It's not fair!"

Perkalicious blinked at her through teary eyes. Annie stopped her self-pitying tirade to study the woman. She'd—

Well, hell. She must be up ten pounds, easy, Annie realized.

"There's something wrong with this plan," Annie said.

Perkalicious replied with a sad little nod. Annie sighed, collected her things, and went out to the meeting area.

Dee moved her purse so Annie could sit down. "Well? How'd we do?"

"Don't ask," Annie spat. "I'm done."

"You're kidding. You're up?"

"Almost eight pounds. *Eight pounds!* I gained a baby in one week!"

"I don't get it." Dee shook her head. "Are you hiding something from me? Buying ice cream cakes in secret?" She rushed out her next words before Annie could think of a rude response. "So, rumor has it that Erica's grave was *desecrated* last night. Someone dug her up. She'd only been in the ground one day."

"What?" Annie was shocked out of her weight-gain misery. "Why would someone do that? Was she buried with treasure or something?"

"I can't imagine. Sounds like something out of *Frankenstein*," Dee said with a shudder. "Where's Katrina? Do you see her?"

Annie scanned the crowd, which was decidedly sparser tonight, but didn't see the redhead. "Not here, I guess."

"I'm going to text her. I'm not going to let both of you quit on me. If she's out, you're staying. I'll pay your meeting fee."

"But it's just not *working*, Dee."

"Listen, I didn't want to mention it, but I'm down another pound. If you want to lose weight, I suggest you seriously consider the Tootsie Roll method of point-counting."

Annie sighed as she let herself into the house. She felt defeated and fat.

"Thank God you're home," Doug called out. "Come here and help me."

She found Doug in the La-Z-Boy, struggling to get up. "I'm stuck," he admitted with a blush. "Pull me out." Annie grabbed his hands and leaned back, using her weight as a counterbalance to help him out of the chair. For a moment, he didn't budge, but with an animal growl from the back of his throat, he heaved himself forward and broke free. "Thanks," he puffed. "That may have been the single most humiliating moment of my life."

"We're going to the grocery store tomorrow," Annie said. "You're going to start counting points with me. No more vegetables and pita breads. We're buying Tootsie Rolls."

"I'm game," Doug said, and padded upstairs after her.

Annie agreed to meet Dee for coffee on Monday after receiving a cryptic voicemail from her friend. She rushed in after work and found Dee sitting in a dark corner of the Dunkin' Donuts, cradling two cups of coffee. Dee slid a cup toward Annie as she sat down.

"There's non-fat, sugar-free vanilla creamer in there. Zero points. Katrina's gone," Dee said, her voice low.

"What do you mean, gone?" Annie took a sip. Disgusting. Exactly how she expected diet creamer to taste. She took another swallow.

"I mean she's no longer with us. She never texted me back, so I called her on Friday. Left a voicemail. Called again yesterday. Her sister called me back last night. Katrina . . . her sister found her at home, sitting at the kitchen table, facedown in a giant salad platter. Said it looked like Katrina had eaten herself to death." Dee's mouth twitched down at the corner. "Christ, how does someone even *do* that?"

"What the hell is going on?" Annie said. "Erica, and now Katrina? Two women we knew from Weight Watchers, both fairly young, and now they're both dead. I mean, neither one of them looked *good* the last time I saw them, but still . . . I don't get it. Is there some sort of killer superflu going around?" She made a mental note to check and make sure she and Doug had both gotten their flu shots.

"I'm working on a theory," Dee said. "But I don't think you're gonna like it."

"Try me."

"Think about it. Everyone at the meetings has been putting on weight. Like, *alarming* weight. Which doesn't make sense, because if there's one thing I know about this plan, it's that it works. No matter how many times they change it. If you stick to the diet, you lose *weight*, gosh darn it."

"Yeah, well, maybe *you* do. But it doesn't seem to be working for all of us."

"But that's the thing. Like I said, I've been going to meetings pretty much all my life. Whenever I get so big that I can't stand myself, I join a group again. Been doing that for forty years now, give or take. And when the plan doesn't work for someone, there's always a reason. They're nibbling when they're making dinner and not counting the points. Or they're guessing at points values or portions, and they're guessing wrong. I knew one woman, back in the days before points, who used to count one jelly doughnut as two breads and a fruit. Or someone struggles with the plan, then finds out they have an underactive thyroid. There's always a *reason* why it doesn't work."

"Well, it's not working. I'm not eating doughnuts and my thyroid was just fine the last time I had blood work done. It has to be the plan."

"It's not the plan," Dee said. "I think it's the vegetables."

"What? That doesn't make any sense. Veggies are zero points—everyone knows that!"

"Think about it. You've been bringing in stuff from your garden for a month now. As soon as you did, people started gaining weight." Dee took a breath. "Except me."

"And you didn't take any of the vegetables? Not one cucumber?"

"Nothing." Dee quickly touched her forehead and shoulders in the sign of the cross.

"Vegetables that make you fat? That's like—well, it's the ultimate betrayal!"

"You didn't happen to put your garden on top of an ancient Indian burial ground, did you?"

Annie thought about the blue radishes. The green beans, gnarled like arthritic witches' fingers. The cucumber hydra. "Well, there *is* something weird going on with my garden. I'll give you that."

"Weird how?"

"Maybe you should come over and take a look."

The garden had started to decay with Annie's neglect. The cucumber vines had withered, leaving yellowed, pearly cylinders rotting in the dirt. The tomato plants were stooped, their fruit blackened with rot.

"What are those?" Dee asked, pointing to a row of graying bushes with powdery white dust on their leaves.

"Spaghetti squash. I completely forgot I put those in." Annie stepped cautiously over the dying cucumbers to inspect the plants. She squatted, then lifted up an oval, golden squash. "Want one?"

Dee squinted. Annie moved closer. Dee's face drained of blood, and she took a step backward.

"Stop. Put that down. Slow, Annie. Real slow."

"What's your problem?" Annie looked at the spaghetti squash in her hand. It looked brighter than the ones she'd seen in the store, sure, maybe a little bigger—

The squash was pulsing.

Annie shrieked and let go, thinking *ohgodohgodohgod* as she watched it fall and crack open with a horrifying *ker-chunk*. The innards exploded in a squirming, squealing knot. Annie was still wearing her dress shoes from work. She started stomping on wormlike creatures, yelling and tramping until the stringy pulp stopped moving. She checked the bottoms of her shoes. Yellow bits of viscera clung to her soles.

What were you expecting? Blood? She giggled. Her laughter sounded high-pitched and on the verge of hysterical.

"Theory doesn't seem so crazy now, does it?" Dee said, leading her friend into the house.

They found Doug in the kitchen, standing in front of the refrigerator with the door open as if trying to cool down on a hot summer day.

"What're you doing?" Annie's voice was still shrill from the scare in the garden.

"I'm hungry," Doug said. He looked at Dee and held out a hand. "I'm Doug." He turned to Annie. "We have any of that cucumber salad left?"

"No!" Annie snapped. "We aren't eating one more thing from Satan's garden! Here," she said, snatching a bag of marshmallows off the kitchen table. "Eat these."

"Good choice," Dee murmured. "You can have two for only one p—"

"I don't give a hoot about points right now! Did you *see* that thing? That squash was alive!" Annie started crying, her voice hitching.

"What the hell are you talking about, woman?"

Annie huddled behind Doug, using him as a shield as he approached the spaghetti squash bushes. Dee pointed at the offending vegetables with a flashlight from behind the deer netting. Doug was holding a butane gas torch, its blue flame steady in the twilight. He crouched down next to a nest of yellow orbs.

"Okay, ladies, the joke's on me. Ha ha." He stood up, frowning.

"Maybe they're sleeping," Dee said in a tiny voice.

"She might be right, Doug. I'm telling you, the darn things were throbbing. Crack one open if you don't believe us." She stepped back.

"Here goes," Doug said, plucking a squash from the vine. He smashed it down against the ground.

The vegetable rocked briefly, then settled on the grass.

"It split right open before," Dee murmured. "That makes no—oh my word, are they *learning*? Adapting? Is that even—"

"Stomp on it! You have to crack it *open*!" Annie said, cutting her off.

Doug lifted a booted heel and brought it down. The oblong vessel exploded with a squawk of indignant fury. Wriggling, buttery tresses of squash innards wrestled to escape the light of Dee's shaky flashlight.

"Oh, holy crapshooters! What the fuuuuu—"

"The flamethrower! Hit 'em with the torch!"

Doug gave the knob on the side of the flamethrower a hard turn, causing the blue finger of fire to elongate. He aimed it at the squirming mass, then began moving his arm wider, setting the whole garden on fire. Vines popped and howled as the fire caught and grew.

"The shed," Annie said, her eyes widening in the glow. The flames grew taller; angrier; she thought she could hear the plants screaming.

"Screw the shed. I'll build another one."

"But the rototiller. Isn't there gas?"

"Shoot. I'll go grab the extinguisher."

The three of them sat at the kitchen table, silent except for the occasional rustle as Dee fished out another marshmallow from the bag.

"Okay," Doug finally said. "We need to figure out what we just witnessed."

"Have we definitively ruled out Indian burial ground?" Dee asked.

"It's not the land. Doug and I have planted gardens there before. It's—I think it was the fertilizer. It *has* to be. That's the only thing we did differently this time."

"Well, we've gotta go find that old farmer. Warn him," Doug said.

"He's staying at Ned Ellis's farm, I think. By the cemetery. It's kind of late. We can go over there tomorrow."

"No, we should go now," Doug said. "What if he's fighting his own army of demonic tomatoes as we speak? We need to get over there." He pushed back from the table, his chair scraping the hardwood floor. "Let me grab the flamethrower, and we'll get going."

Night was firmly upon them as they pulled onto the dusty dirt road that led to the silhouette of a silo in the distance. A farmhouse with black windows watched their arrival. "I don't think anyone's home," Annie whispered.

"Why are you whispering?" Doug said.

"I don't want to alert the plants that we're here."

"Good point."

Doug climbed out of the car, closing his door softly. Annie and Dee scrabbled out after him. The women flanked him. Shadowy rows of corn rose up to their left, stalks standing rigid like soldiers. Annie shuddered. Doug held a finger to his lips, then pointed.

A light was on in one of the inky silhouettes. A barn?

The three crept toward the building, matching their paces. *Like we're off to see the wizard*, Annie thought. Her soft snort of laughter earned her a poke in the side from Doug.

They crept to the barn, then Doug tugged them down to crouch beneath an open window. He lifted his head slowly, peeked over the sill, then ducked back down. "I can't see anything. You look."

Annie slowly straightened, peering into the barn. She let her eyes adjust for a minute. The interior looked almost bare, save for the dirt dusting the floor and the cobwebs clinging to the walls. A huge porcelain tub loomed in the center of the room, with a metal arm that hooked up into a vat. It was churning. The whole contraption looked like a giant electric mixer. The smell hit her: cat urine, raisins, and decay. *Making more fertilizer?* she thought, then: *not with those red stains dribbling down the side. Wine?* She moved to the next window a little further down, hoping for a better angle.

A flash of movement made her bob down, but after a moment, she peeked up again. Someone was on the far side of the tub; someone not tall enough for her to quite see over the rim, though she could see what they were doing: throwing things up and over into the vat. *A mannequin's arm*, Annie thought at first. A foot. A mud-caked head and neck, the muck only partially obscuring a large blue butterfly on the decapitated neck. Annie clapped a hand over her mouth. *Katrina!*

She caught a glimpse of the top of a bronzed, freckled scalp bobbing behind the far side of the vat. She squinted, studying the hands tossing the pieces in the brew like a witch at her cauldron. Thick, calloused hands that resembled nothing so much as a bear's paws.

She slid back down against the wall, then crawled back to Doug and Dee on her hands and knees. "We have a problem," she whispered shakily, trying to fight the urge to scream and run. "It's him. Farmer Paul. He's—he's—" Charlton Heston popped in her head. *Soylent Green is people!*

Dee and Doug said nothing. She jostled Doug with her elbow. "Hey!" She connected with something hard. Coarse.

Like a vine.

Dee's flashlight lay forgotten on the grass by their feet. Annie fumbled for it, then brought it up to shine on her husband's face. Doug's cheeks were purple and bloated. Tight, spiky vines—*cucumber? No, pumpkin*, the rational part of

Annie's mind theorized—were wound around his neck, loop after loop, in a stranglehold. His open, gaping maw told of his last attempt to scream—maybe to warn Annie, the words cut short before he could get them out.

Dee was next to him. Woody tendrils encased her head, her mouth, her throat. She might have tried to cry out, too, but shoot after shoot of ropy fingers were crammed into her mouth, choking her silent. Annie crab-walked backward, trying to put space between herself and the horror. Her head thumped against the wooden slats of the barn.

A tug on her shoe. Creeping tendrils wound up her leg.

Annie shrieked, pounding at the vines with the flashlight. "Off! Get—off!" she shouted, but they continued to snake upward, reaching her torso, looping coils around her with the speed and grace of an anaconda.

"Zero points!" the old farmer cackled from somewhere above her. She jerked her head up and saw him peering over the sill she'd just been watching him through. "Told you my fertilizer would do wonders for your garden! *And* my wallet," he added. "Amazing stuff, really. Best part is, it perpetuates itself. You crazy dieters will do *anything* to lose a pound. I mean, really, lady—who eats a blue radish? Didn't that set off any alarm bells for you?" Annie opened her mouth to respond, but the vines pulled tight against her torso, making it hard to even draw a breath. "So you eat the poisoned fruits of the vine, and all I have to do is wait for your loved ones to pay their respects and plant you in the ground. Then *I* dig you up, and start the process all over again." He winked.

Annie wanted to reach up and pluck that wink right out of his eye. But the ropy plant was up to her neck, and a soft leaf cupped her chin, as if to say *Hey, pay attention to* me *now*.

She turned her head. The vine reared back, as if to show off the perfectly symmetrical, fiery pumpkin cocked before her face. The lines in the impossibly bright orange flesh were pulled to the sides a bit, as if the pumpkin itself was sneering at her.

"Eat your vegetables," the farmer said with a hiss.

She did.

HUNGRY MAN

How's it going? Cooper texted.

It's a memorial service, **Jodi** replied. How do u think?

I hate those things.

Who doesn't?

U hanging in there?

Yeah. It's not *my* mom, so not like I'm emotionally traumatized R anything. I feel bad for Lindsey. She keeps cracking jokes, then breaking down & crying every 5 min. I miss u. Hate being here.

I offered to come with.

I know & thanks. But u don't know anyone here. Hell, I don't know anyone here, really. I haven't seen these people since we all graduated HS 15 yrs ago.

Want me to call with an emergency?

Tempting . . .

From Jodi, five minutes later: Things r looking up! The Conner twins just showed up with their dad. I haven't seen Mr. C in years. Gonna go chat him up.

Well, it's official. Mr. C has completely lost his mind.

From Cooper: ?

Mr. C used 2 B a live-off-the-land hunter and fisherman, u know? Always stopping by the house to drop off a container of goose stew or a lb of venison burger. My point is he was, like, old school New England. Maybe a little scary because he was gruff, but he was the neighborhood parent who ALWAYS watched out for us kids.

The crazy hunter? Cooper had heard Jodi's occasional story. That *is* cool that he's there then.

Ah, no. I just spent 30 min listening to him talk about his psychic. Not kidding. One of the guys at his moose lodge or whatever has "the gift" according to Mr. C.

Can u escape? Go to bathroom or something?

Already tried that. Mr. C was waiting for me outside the door. Says there's a reason for everything and he's trying 2 figure out why we're reconnecting now, at this point in life.

Cuz your friend's mom died, and u all lived in the same neighborhood? It's a funeral. Seems pretty obvs. Did you tell him he's prolly next?

HAHAHA NO. I'm gonna go find I of the twins and see if they can get their dad away from me. Think I see Helena by the bar.

Eight minutes later, from Jodi: Funny, I don't recall Helena Conner being such a bitch in high school.

You leaving any time soon? Should I eat lunch without you?

Nothing for ten minutes. Cooper was freakin' starving, and when she didn't respond right away, he started to hope Jodi was on her way. Maybe she'd even stopped at KFC to pick up a bucket of extra crispy to eat at the house. His stomach grumbled its approval, but his heart sank when the wavy ellipsis bubble popped up on the phone screen. Jodi would never type and drive.

Eat without me. I can't even right now.

Why? What's going on?

I don't even know how I got roped into this. I have to drive Mr. C home—except, of course, he's insisting I stop by the lodge with him to meet his psychic. There's some sort of stupid game dinner going on tonight and a bunch are there preparing the food right now.

Why can't one of the twins do it? Cooper's eyes pricked with tears as his dreams of fried chicken disappeared in a cloud of moose-lodge smoke.

Hannah disappeared, like, 5 min after she got here. Made sure she was seen by the grieving family, then poof! Out. Wish I'd thought of that. Helena just left with her husband.

Who ditches their dad at a memorial service?

These jerkbags, that's who. In Helena's defense, she *did* thank me for driving her dad home. That's when I found out I was driving him home.

Call him an Uber.

Can't. Mr. C is now convinced the reason why we met up again today is so I can meet this psychic. That the Great and Powerful Oz must have a message for me.

Cooper paused, his thumb hovering over the phone. He *thought* he knew his girlfriend of ten months pretty well, but still . . . U don't really believe that tho, do u? He hit the send key and hoped he hadn't just committed some sort of egregious offense.

Cooper watched the wavy ellipsis for a full minute before Jodi's response came through. R U f'n kidding me right now? I just want to come HOME! But what am I supposed to do? I've known this man my whole life. When I was 6 & fell out of a tree in the field behind our cul-de-sac, it was Mr. C who found me and brought me to the hospital. I owe him. He's like, 80 & delusional now.

Cooper sighed. How long you think you'll be?

Dunno. Hoping an hr, max? Thirty seconds later, a second message: Make that more like 2. Mr. C's lodge is in Madison. So figure 40 min driving time each way, plus I have to be polite and meet his psychic friend. Though I do expect he knows we're coming, hahaha.

Cooper checked the time on his phone, then thumbed up a new contact: Anna, the payroll clerk from work he'd been sleeping with for over a month now. U around? I just got 2 hrs suddenly free.

Her response was immediate: *Come on over.*

He grinned. Anna's place was only a ten-minute drive. If he stopped at the KFC on the way, fifteen.

From Anna's parking lot, he shot Jodi a quick message: Heading out for food. Let me know how it's going. That would cover him if he didn't respond right away to any texts she might send.

It was a good fifty-five minutes before Cooper's phone dinged with a new message. U there? By that time, he and Anna had already gotten naked, done filthy, wonderful things to each other, and were eating crispy chicken and potato wedges in the afterglow.

Anna sighed. "The warden?"

"Yup. Sorry." He typed back: Here. What's up?

Surrounded by crazy old men. How do I get out of this?

He licked his fingers, wiped them off on Anna's bed sheets, and shrugged. "Seems to me you asked for it," he murmured, but typed instead, I got nothing. Just grin & bear it?

Anna leaned over and started gently tickling his chest, in that way that signaled she was ready for round two, and he set the phone aside without waiting for a response.

"Ah, crap," he said a half hour later. He'd missed Jodi's reply to his grin-and-bear-it advice: Can u call me? He pulled on his boxers, then his jeans, throwing Anna an apologetic look as he held a finger to his lips in the universal sign for "shush." Then he called Jodi. It went right to voicemail.

Sorry, was driving home from KFC, he texted. He'd found the easiest lies to keep straight were based in small truths, and if she quizzed him about lunch, he'd remember the wedges. Just tried calling. U ok?

No response. He fought with his shirt, getting the neck caught temporarily on the bridge of his nose before getting it all the way on with one last tug.

"Everything okay?" Anna asked, but she sounded irritated.

"I don't know. She's not answering, and she's with a weird old man." He forced himself to slow down, sitting on the corner of the bed to pull on his socks. He didn't want to upset his side piece by babbling too much about his girlfriend. "You?"

"Oh, I'm a-okay," Anna said. "Thanks for coming over."

It was her way of dismissing him. For once he was grateful for the brush-off.

In the car in Anna's parking lot, he tried again. This time, Jodi picked up, but the signals where she was couldn't have been very good, because the call failed before she got a word out. He'd already opened Safari and was Googling moose lodges in Madison when the text came: Sorry about that. Spotty service here. Met the psychic.

Warm relief coursed through him like a shot of whiskey. How'd it go?

About as expected. He def said some totally generic stuff, like "U recently experienced a loss." Who hasn't? I figure he meant my cute black boots with the cracked sole.

Yes, that *was* a tragic loss.

Plus I'm almost sure Mr. C mentioned we'd just come from a memorial service. But the guy got some stuff right on, too.

Like what?

He said u had chicken for lunch.

Cooper swallowed hard, then chuckled. Chicken was, like, the most popular meat in the country, wasn't it? Cool was all he could think to reply. Then: On ur way home now?

Not yet. They're insisting I stay for the game dinner. I won't, but Mr. C missing so I can't find him to lie and tell him I'm deathly ill & have to go.

I'm staking out men's room door so I can accost him when he exits. Pull his trick from the mem svc on him & C how he likes it.

A pause, then a second text bubble: Psychic also said u're cheating on me.

"Turds in a can of stewed turds!" Cooper exclaimed. Had she believed the man? "Answer fast, or she'll *really* get suspicious," he advised himself, a prick of sweat blossoming on his forehead as he typed. Don't be ridiculous. Think he meant I cheated by getting chicken without u? Maybe she'd buy that. I'm right here at home all alone, waiting 4 u. He scanned the parking lot guiltily.

At first glance, the lot was still, but then he caught movement off to his right that made his heart catch in his throat. For one wild moment he thought it was Jodi, not outside some moose lodge men's room waiting to pounce on a senile old loony-tune when he emerged and shout that she had to go, but somehow impossibly *here*, catching him red-handed in his web of lies. The panic subsided as his eyes tracked the movement: an old, stooped man with thick glasses and a white goatee lurched along the sidewalk, leaning heavily on a thick cane for support. Unless this was the famed Mr. C, sent to spy on him by a faceless moose lodge psychic, Cooper figured Anna was still safely his secret. He gave a nervous chuckle—Jodi's dumb psychic was getting under his skin. But how had the guy known . . . ?

"Lucky guess. Don't protest too much. Casually change the topic," he murmured, typing away fervently. Think Mr. C's trying to pull the old "duck into the bathroom and maybe they'll go away" ploy?

LOL Maybe. I'll wait maybe 10 more, then I'm out of here.

Perfect. That'd give Cooper plenty of time to get home, hop in the shower to get the smell of sex off him, then throw a load of laundry—including the clothes he now wore—in the machine. He'd be twenty minutes into an episode of *Ted Lasso* by the time she walked through the door.

Sounds good, he replied. What does the psychic say we're having 4 dinner?

He thought he was being clever, but as he waited for a reply, bouncing his knee and fighting the urge to start driving before she answered, he second-guessed his text. Did the question make it sound like he believed in the psychic? Was it somehow an admittance of his affair? He wanted to turn the engine over, take off and rush home to scrub away the evidence as soon as possible, but if she responded while he was driving, and he didn't answer right away, she'd know he wasn't where he'd said he was. "C'mon, c'mon . . ." he muttered, eyeing the old man with the cane, still shuffling along the sidewalk, though much closer now.

Cooper gasped as White Goatee tumbled to the ground. Cooper blinked, then opened the car door without thinking twice. He tucked his cell phone in his back pocket and was by the fallen man's side in four long strides. "Let me help," Cooper said. "Here, take my hands—we'll get you up. Are you okay?"

"My hip!" the older man barked, waving off Cooper's proffered palms. He squirmed around on the sidewalk, his cane underneath his body. "I popped it out of its socket, I think. Beans!"

"Okay. Sure, yeah. Let me call someone." Cooper pulled out his phone, then hesitated. If he called for an ambulance, would he have to go *with* this guy? He tried to think up a plausible lie, a new one to explain why he'd gone to the hospital with a stranger. Nothing came to mind. He'd just have to tell the EMTs he wasn't riding with them, Cooper decided. His cell phone screen showed that Jodi still hadn't responded to his last text. "Not that it matters, I guess. *She's* not in a hurry to get home." A twist of worry squeezed his stomach. Where *was* she, anyway?

He glanced down at the old man again, and to his surprise, found that White Goatee seemed to have recovered quickly. He'd worked the cane out from under him, and was now on his knees. He held the cane almost like a rifle, and when Cooper leaned over to help him the rest of the way up, the man tapped the base of the cane in the center of Cooper's chest.

"Woah, there. I'm just trying to help," Cooper said with a grin, palms up in surrender, his phone still in his right hand, 9-1-1 still uncalled. "What's going on?"

"Jeez, you're slow, kid," White Goatee said. "Though Henry said you would be. That's my psychic—just unbelievable, that guy. The real deal. I mean, he said you were cheating on Jodi, sent me here to spy on you, and here you are."

"Wait—what? That was my *joke* guess!"

"I've known Jodi since she was knee high to a grasshopper. How dare you cheat on that sweet girl?" A chill seized Cooper's veins as he realized the handle of the cane was no such thing, but rather a hammer and trigger. Which meant the end tapping his shirt—

—the explosion was muffled against his chest. Cooper's heart stopped pumping before he even hit the ground.

Mr. C fumbled for Cooper's cell phone, catching it before it could land and shatter, and it was he who read Jodi's delayed response: Psychic says we're having *u* 4 dinner.

THE DEVIL'S IN THE DETAILS

This pesky demonic possession thing is my own fault. I never should've been playing with that Ouija board.

We were all sleeping over at Tiffany's house. It was Friday, the day before Tiff's sixteenth birthday. Me, the birthday girl, Allison, plus Gretchen and Gigi—identical twins—were up way past midnight. Tiffany's mom had rented *Children of the Corn* from Blockbuster Video, and after watching that, none of us could get to sleep.

"Open my gift now," Allison said. "We can use it tonight."

Tiffany was particularly hard to shop for. Her parents bought her everything she wanted, as soon as she asked. She was the first one of us to have a cellphone—a sweet 1995 Nokia Bananaphone, which she had in her manicured hands less than a week after the phone hit the market. With her corkscrew perm and wardrobe purchased exclusively at The Gap, there was nothing Tiffany didn't have. I couldn't imagine what

Allison might have found for a gift. I'd gotten Tiffany the cassette of *Jagged Little Pill*, which I suspected she would never listen to. It was better than nothing, though.

"Okay, I'll open just one present now." Tiffany beamed as she tore through Allison's carefully taped ladybug wrapping paper, then squealed. "A wee-gee board!"

"It's wee-*juh*," Gigi said with a sniff. She and her sister looked exactly alike, save for a side ponytail in their long brown hair that Gigi liked to wear on the left, Gretchen on the right—I think—and I often mixed the two of them up. But Gigi was the one with the obnoxious habit of correcting everyone else's grammar, so I knew it was her.

"Call it whatever you want," I said. "Just open it up and let's try it!"

"Don't encourage her, Julie. Guys, are you sure we should?" Gretchen asked, her voice tiny. She was, in any situation, the total wuss of the pair, so again, I knew it was her.

"Don't be such a baby," Gigi scoffed. "Of course we should. I need to find out if I'm going to marry Travis Pullman." Travis Pullman was a junior, one year ahead of us, and played center for the school's hockey team. He was tall and blond, with deep dimples and a quick smile—easily the best-looking guy on the whole Tomahawks team. I think we were *all* kind of hoping the spirit board would name us as Travis's future bride.

Tiffany pulled the cellophane from the Ouija box and unpacked the board. "Shouldn't we light some candles or something?" Allison asked. "To get the atmosphere right?"

"My mom has some fancy candles in the cabinet over the refrigerator," Tiffany said, examining the heart-shaped piece of wood that the spirits would use to point to letters and spell out messages on the board. Allison padded off to the kitchen, and returned with a glowing green candle in a jar. The sickly sweet smell of artificial peppermint filled the living room. Tiffany laid the board on the carpet, and we all sat cross-legged around it—except Gretchen, who planted herself on the couch and refused to join our circle. "Okay," Tiffany announced, suddenly an expert. This was no surprise—she could be really bossy. "Everybody put two fingers on the planchette."

"The what?" Gigi asked. *Score one for Tiffany over the grammar queen*, I thought.

"The pointer," Tiffany said, her pink polished fingernails resting on the smooth wooden piece. "Everybody has to touch it, but nobody move it." Tentatively, we all placed our fingers on the pointer, some of us giggling nervously. Gigi burped and accidentally jostled the device.

"Don't move it!" Tiffany barked. She cleared her throat. "Spirits," she intoned solemnly. "Spirits, come to us. Answer our questions from beyond the grave." I couldn't look at her while she was talking, or else I'd crack up.

"Spirits?" Tiffany said again. "Are you there?"

The planchette began to move, inching up to the YES printed on the upper left-hand corner of the board. "Are you guys pushing it? You're pushing it," she huffed.

Gretchen squirmed from the safety of the couch. "Guys, I don't think you should mess around with that. Remember when we rented *Witchboard*? And an evil spirit totally possessed that redhead? I wish you guys would stop."

Allison hesitated at Gretchen's words, twisting a lock of her own auburn hair nervously. "I hadn't thought of that," she admitted.

"Allison, put your fingers back on the planchette! And Gretchen, don't be such a friggin' baby," Tiffany snapped, but

Gretchen would not be shamed into silence.

"Look at the movie we just watched. Isaac was possessed by the devil and came back from the dead to get Malachai. That could happen to one of you!"

Gigi, who had made it a habit to deride her sister whenever possible, snorted in disgust. "Okay, Gretchen. I'm *so* sure. If you don't shut up, when I get possessed by Satan, I'm gonna come after you, got it?" Gretchen shut up, but remained pouting, arms wrapped around herself.

"Oh, spirits from beyond," Tiffany started again, "We ask you to come to us and tell us your secrets. Tell us who, for instance, Travis Pullman really has the hots for." The planchette slowly slid to a letter. T, then I, then F—

"You're moving it, Tiffany!" Gigi said, tugging the pointer toward the G.

"Am not!" Tiffany said, pulling the planchette back to F.

"Cut it out, you two! I thought we were trying to have a serious séance here," Allison whined. Tiffany and Gigi glowered at each other, but pushed the planchette back to the middle. "Spirits?" Allison asked. "We promise to behave now. We await your messages from beyond." The pointer twitched. Then it scraped out a message across the board, Allison whispering each letter as it moved.

"I. W-A-N . . . T-Y-O-U . . . R-S-O-U-L." Alison looked confused. "What?"

"I want your soul," I said. I was feeling a little embarrassed. The whole Ouija experience had been pretty silly so far. I hoped Travis Pullman would never find out about our little séance, because then he'd think we were all too stupid to date. "Okay. Got it," I joked. "Come on in, then, demon, and possess me. I'm game."

Not, as it turns out, the smartest thing I've ever said.

What I *thought* happened next was that I'd taken a little nap. After all, it was late, and I wasn't used to staying up past midnight. I jerked awake, still sitting cross-legged, and rubbed my eyes. I blinked a few times, then looked around at the other girls to see if anyone had noticed my quick snooze.

Tiffany was directly across from me. Her perfect corkscrew curls sagged under the weight of what looked like soggy green oatmeal slush, which dripped down the front of her pretty pink baby-doll pajamas. Allison, to my left, sobbed hysterically, wrapping the bottom of her Garfield nightgown around her right forearm. Gigi, to my right, had fat tears running down her red cheeks, but she appeared uninjured. Gretchen still cowered on the couch, holding up two remote controls to form a cross. A dark stain soiled the crotch of her Mickey Mouse jammies.

"What the hell, you guys?" I asked. "What'd I miss?"

"What did you miss? Christ, Julie! What did you *miss*?" Tiffany dragged a hand through the slop in her hair, then shook it at me, splattering oatmeal chunks in my general direction. "I hate you!"

"Hey, chill out! What's your problem?" I wiped a glob of goo off my face. Up close, it smelled foul. "I fell asleep. Did you guys have some sort of, er . . . food fight? What happened?"

Tiffany leveled an icy stare. If looks could kill, my skull would've shattered. "Well, let me fill you in, princess. First, you started talking in this moronic raspy voice, like you were trying to imitate Darth Vader or something. Told us to call you 'Charlie.' Ringing any bells yet?"

I shrugged. "Nope."

"Sure it doesn't. Of course not. Because you were possessed and all. Then you told Gigi that Travis Pullman thought she was a 'contemptuous troll'—I think those were your exact words—and she'd have better luck hitting on a turnip than getting a date with him. Remember now?"

"I would never—" I had to stop to stifle my chuckle. I wasn't quite sure what contemptuous meant, but I was pretty sure Gigi did, and it didn't sound flattering. And a troll? Yeah, I could see that. "Gigi. I would never call you that. I have no idea what Travis thinks of you. And didn't you tell me that just last week he accidentally-on-purpose brushed your arm when you passed him in the hallway?" I tried to keep my voice as innocent-sounding as possible, like the hallway brush was something to get excited about.

Gigi sniffed. "I know you were faking it to get a laugh, but it was still a mean thing to say."

"Faking it?" Allison interrupted. "She bit me! *Bit* me!" She waved her forearm under my nose accusingly. "And then she power-puked all over Tiffany. Faking it, my foot! I can see a playful nip to try and sell an act, but she left tooth marks in my arm! And I know what we ate tonight. Pizza, ice cream, cheese puffs—she didn't barf up any of that. That puke all over Tiffany is green oatmeal. Oatmeal from *Hell*," she hissed.

"You guys are kidding, right? This is some sort of elaborate prank that you decided to pull when you realized I'd conked out. Very funny," I said, but I didn't find it amusing at all. It felt sort of mean, actually.

"Get out! Out of my house!" Tiffany howled. "I thought you were my *friend*!" Gigi nodded in agreement. Allison looked a little sheepish.

I burst into tears. Why were they all being so mean to me? This wasn't just a sick joke anymore. Tiffany was trying to get me ousted from the crowd, permanently.

Allison took pity on me, which I'll admit was pretty big of her considering the forearm bite. She patted my back with her good hand while I phoned my mother in the middle of the night. I couldn't even explain to her what had happened—none of it made any sense. With my mom on her way, I moved over to the couch, sniffling. Gretchen scooted back from me, holding up her remote-control cross in my general direction. "Stay away!" she yelped.

"Oh, come off it, Gretchen. I don't know why you guys are doing this to me, but it's not funny. Possessed by a demon? Named Charlie? Really? *Charlie?*"

You rang? said a voice inside my head, not unlike an otherworldly Darth Vader. He let loose a low rumbling chuckle, and I could feel him in there, *sense* him looking out at Gretchen through my eyes, thinking she would make a tasty snack for a hungry hellhound.

Oh, poop.

Mom was none too pleased about picking me up in the middle of the night, but on the ride home I told her that all the girls had turned on me for falling asleep in the middle of a game. I didn't mention that I'd bitten Allison and target-vomited all over Tiffany. Mom was sympathetic. "I'm so sorry, honey," she murmured as we pulled into the garage. "Teenage girls can be so mean."

Yeah, I thought. *We can.*

Mean? Charlie piped up from his corner of my brain. *You should see the harpies breaking the thorny branches of the suicide trees, you want mean! Not for the weak of stomach, I tell you!*

"Shut up, Charlie," I muttered. I was tired, and not entirely sure I could wrap my mind around the idea that I was potentially demonically possessed. I'd figure everything out in the morning. For now, I just wanted to curl up in my own bed.

The rest of the weekend passed quietly. I left two messages on Tiffany's answering machine, but she never called back. Ditto Gigi and Gretchen. But Allison called to tell me her arm wasn't so bad after all—I hadn't broken skin, but she had an impressive bite-shaped bruise. "I have a big, chunky bracelet hiding it right now. My mom won't ever let me hang out with you again if she sees it," she whispered.

"Allison—you have to believe me—I don't remember any of that at all," I said. I felt awful. "I'm so sorry I chomped on your arm. You know I'd never do that on purpose, right?"

"Oh, I know what I saw." Allison let her voice drop to a whisper. "You were possessed by a demon, all right. Your eyes were all red, and you were foaming at the mouth. I *know* it wasn't you." She sounded a bit dramatic, but I appreciated her words. Maybe Allison and I could break off from the other girls and start our own group of friends.

Allison interrupted my reverie of our cool new clique. "It's gone now, though, right? I mean, the demon left your body after that, right?"

"Um, yeah, I guess. I mean, I haven't heard from him since Friday," I said truthfully.

"He talked to you?" she gasped.

"In my head. A little bit," I admitted.

Let ME talk to that yummy little morsel, Charlie jeered from the vicinity of my inner ear.

"Gotta go!" I said, hanging up on Allison. "Charlie. You're still here," I sighed.

Where else would I be?

"Can I ask why, exactly?" I was feeling a little put out. Plus, I wasn't sure how much access he had to my mind. I mean, sure, he could take over and make me nibble on my best friend, but could he read my thoughts? Specifically, was he aware of my sexy-type thoughts about one Travis Pullman?

Yup, I can see it all, Charlie said. *You want him? I can get him for you.*

"What? No," I snapped. I wanted Travis to fall in love with me for me, not because the demonic entity currently hanging out in my body *made* him. But . . . it was tempting. No. "Stop making me lose focus, Charlie. Why are you here?"

To take over the world and bring about the end of days, so my great dark father, Beelzebub, can rise to his ultimate power and torment the souls of everyone, for all eternity, Charlie said. *I thought that was a given. That's pretty much a demon's job description.*

"Oh. Yeah, sure. Tormenting souls. Makes sense. Sorry," I said. "But, um, realistically, how do you expect to make this happen trapped inside of me? I mean, I can't even figure out how to get rid of the giant zit on my chin. And don't say spray Windex on it—I tried that already. My point is, isn't there anyone a little more qualified to help you with your evil plan?"

You'll do just fine, Charlie said. *First up, though, let's take care of that pimple.* And with that, Charlie went to work.

When I got to school on Monday morning, I was a whole new girl.

Charlie, for all of his jabbering about Satan's rise and ultimate dominion over the souls of the world, had some pretty cool tricks up his sleeve. He not only got rid of that giant zit, he smoothed out my skin to a porcelain sheen, erasing the moles on my arms and freckles on my chest. My hair, which had previously been limp, listless, and an unfortunate shade of dishwater blonde, was now wavy and full, with golden highlights snaking through, so that I looked like a model in a shampoo commercial. And I've always thought my hips were just a bit too wide—inherited from my mother's side of the family, all big-hipped women. Charlie scoffed at me when I mentioned it, but he did slim them down a bit. He lengthened my legs and filled out my chest just enough to make me feel my bra was actually doing its job for once. Charlie and I went through my closet and finally agreed on a pink tank top and denim mini-skirt, but I'd insisted on a gray cardigan to cover up a bit. He grumbled, but finally agreed when I reminded him he wouldn't be able to recruit minions for his dark plan if I was sent home from school for violating the dress code. But for the first time in my life, I felt . . . pretty. I was starting to think that this demonic possession thing had gotten a bad rap. Even Travis did a double take when I passed him on the way to English class. I mentally thanked Charlie, who responded with a modest *'twas nothing*, but it wasn't nothing. I'd never been noticed before in my life. It was something, and I liked it.

Allison sidled up to me on my way to class. "Nice try," she whispered. "That demon's not gone."

"What ever could you mean?" I asked, smiling brightly.

"You look so good, even *I* can't keep my eyes off of you," she said, "and I'm as straight as they come. Watch out for Gigi—she saw you this morning, and she isn't pleased."

"Why? What's her problem?"

"I think she saw Travis checking you out. She didn't like it."

Charlie snickered in the recesses of my mind, but I shrugged it off. "I can't help who he looks at," I said, and Charlie and I headed off to second period.

We hit a bit of a snag in English class. Miss Fotino announced that we'd each be doing a report on our favorite author from the early twentieth century. "The options are endless," she trilled, as we all sat stone-faced, dismayed at the prospect of standing in front of the class to deliver a monotone report. "Forster, Joyce, Mann, Woolf—"

"Virginia Woolf was an arrogant pismire whose wisest action was to transform herself into fish bait for the almighty Zoth-Ommog!" Charlie boomed. I was mortified—and unable to stop my own tongue. "That she was ripped apart by the tentacles of the Dweller in the Depths should come as a relief to all," he added.

Miss Fotino stared at me for a moment—as did everyone in the class, as I sunk lower in my seat—and broke out in a wide smile. "I'll put you down for Lovecraft, Julie."

After class, I hurried to the girls' room, keeping my eyes trained on the scuffed hallway floor to avoid eye contact. A quick check of the bathroom stalls assured me I was alone. I locked the bathroom door—the stoners who liked to pop in for a quick cigarette would just have to find somewhere else to smoke—and stared at myself in the mirror. "Dammit, Charlie, you can't *do* that!"

Do what? he asked, and forced me to blink my eyes in innocence.

"You know exactly what I mean. Spouting crap about Zoo-gog and tentacles whenever you feel like it."

Charlie shrugged my shoulders. *I speak the truth*, he said. *Virginia Woolf was a miserable shrew.*

"Discretion," I spat. "You've gotta cool it, or we'll wind up in a nuthouse. Can't take over the world from there, can you?"

Look at you, Charlie said. *Your hair's a mess.* He took control of my arms, smoothed out my hair and pursed my lips. *Got any lip gloss in your bag?* I didn't.

"Why does it matter?" I asked. Charlie started shrugging off my cardigan, but I wrestled with him, pulling it back up my shoulders. "What are you doing?"

We're going to go find that hockey player you've been lusting after, he said, and I felt an alarming surge of his strength as he seized control of my arms and yanked off my sweater, tying it around my waist.

"Charlie, c'mon! There's a protocol to these things. It takes months of smiling in the hallways, occasionally flipping one's hair back . . . there's subtle eye contact involved," I floundered.

You're taking too long, Charlie said. *I have no time for games.*

I watched as Charlie reached out with my hand, unlocked the lavatory door and pushed us out, slamming full-on into Travis Pullman's broad chest. *How did you know he was there?* I mentally asked Charlie.

I could smell his cologne, Charlie said. *Now smile at him!*

"Oops! Sorry!" I blustered nervously. I'd dropped my notebook when I bumped into Travis. He bent down and retrieved it for me.

"Hey, Julie. You look nice today."

"Thanks," I squeaked, and turned to go on my way. My eyes

locked on Gigi, who was leaning against a row of lockers, shooting me a death stare.

Don't worry about that little troll, Charlie said. *Just jealous is all. She'll get hers.*

To my surprise, when I was walking to catch the bus home after my last class, Travis jogged up next to me. "Want a ride?" he said, a little out of breath.

"Um, me? Really?" I looked around to see if he was talking to someone hotter.

"Yeah, you," he said, flashing me those dimples. "I was gonna cruise over to the mall—wanna come with?"

Boy, did I wanna come with, but I figured I should at least call my mother and get per—"Love to," Charlie growled on my behalf, and Travis cocked his head at me questioningly.

I cleared my throat. "Sure," I said, and followed him to his Civic.

On the drive to the mall, Travis asked me about my favorite bands, if I'd seen any good movies, and if I watched *Xena.* Thank goodness Charlie stepped back and let me answer, or I might've sworn that I loved Detroit crunk metal and considered the villainous Ares the real hero on *Xena.* We pulled up outside Ruby Tuesday. "Figured we could get something to eat first," Travis said.

After placing our order, I noticed Travis studying me intently. "You look different," he said. "Sexier."

Uh-oh. Mom had warned me that boys were only after one thing. "Oh?" I sniffed. I started to unwrap the cardigan from my waist. Time to cover up.

Charlie wrestled for control, forcing me to let go of the sweater and drop my arms lest Travis think I was having a seizure. *Leave it be*, Charlie hissed.

"You know, Gigi Baker told me the craziest story this afternoon," Travis said with a chuckle. "She said—she said you guys were playing with a Ouija board, and you got possessed by an evil spirit."

That cow! I wanted to strangle her for opening her big mou—"That's it! That vile hobgoblin will be the *first* to be sacrificed to the Dark Lord!" Charlie roared. I clamped a hand over my mouth before Charlie could continue.

"Wow," Travis said, staring at me like a hungry kid eyeballing a candy bar. "It's true."

"What's true?" I said casually, pretending that I hadn't just spouted off about dark lords and sacrifice.

"You *are* possessed by a demon. Your eyes just went all red and your voice—there's no way you could be faking that. Sounded like your throat was being scorched by hellfire. That is—*so* cool!" He reached across the table and held my hand.

Looks like your boyfriend is a bit of a dark character himself, Charlie murmured. *Good.*

I quickly gave up on trying to hide Charlie's existence from Travis. There was really no point, and I couldn't get the darn demon to shut up, anyway. Charlie laid out his plans for plunging the world into eternal torment and servitude to Satan, and Travis nodded agreeably. "Sign me up," he said.

"What?" I interjected.

"My parents made me go to Catholic CCD classes every week for ten years. I can't begin to tell you how preachy and boring they were." He smiled. "Time for a little payback."

"Travis, do you hear yourself?" I piped up, mentally pushing Charlie aside. "He's talking about enslaving the world to do the bidding of Satan. Satan! You know, like, the biggest bad guy ever? This is not 'a little payback.' We're talking about hellfire and brimstone and tentacles," I said. I didn't quite have a grasp on Charlie's hellish vision, but I knew it didn't sound good.

"Yeah, I got it. But I don't think you get how mind-numbingly awful CCD class was," he said.

I was starting to suspect that for all of his dimply yumminess, Travis Pullman was not the brightest bulb in the socket.

"We've got to perform an exorcism," Allison said on the phone that night. "I've been doing some research. We'll need an old priest and a young priest."

"Shh! Allison, he's listening. Charlie hears everything I can hear."

I don't mind, Charlie said. *Her silly exorcism plans won't amount to anything. An old priest and a young priest? Is she kidding?*

"Hmm. How about this? I'll set everything up, and just surprise you with it. Sound good?"

"Fine," I said. It was nice to look like a goddess and all, but it was getting a little tiresome having a backseat demon driving half the time. And even though Travis and I had had a pretty steamy make-out session before he dropped me off, I was no longer so sure I wanted to be with a guy who thought eternal damnation on Earth was sensible revenge for after-school religion classes.

Allison was true to her word. When I saw her at school the next day, she only mentioned things like how Mike Tierney had gotten his braces off, and that Amber Deluca and Josh Keller had broken up. No mention of exorcisms at all. I appreciated her efforts, and that she was talking to me at all. Ever since Charlie had made his entrance, I'd lost three friends. Tiffany continued to give me the cold shoulder. Gigi out-and-out hated me. Gretchen ran down the hallway screaming whenever she spotted me. If it weren't for Allison, I'd have no friends left. And as annoying as Tiffany, Gigi, and Gretchen could sometimes be . . . I missed them. I'd found myself feeling wistful when I accidentally said "irregardless" and Gigi wasn't there to correct me.

Don't worry about them, Charlie said. *We don't need them. You have me now.* It was sweet of him to try and cheer me up, being a malignant spirit and all, but it wasn't very comforting.

Travis walked me to and from each class, and sat with me at lunch. I would've been flattered by the attention, but he wanted to talk to Charlie, not me. "So when do we start with the ritual sacrifices? Do they need to be virgins? When do you think Satan will show up?"

"We need an army of dark souls to help us," Charlie said. "Any of your friends have tendencies toward satanic worship?"

"I could probably get the guys on the hockey team to help," Travis mused. "They pretty much do everything I say anyway."

"Perfect," Charlie said. "We can start tonight. We need to find a private place, preferably one with an altar."

"How about the football field? The home team's goal post is decorated right now, since we won the state championship. It kind of looks like an altar."

"It'll have to do," Charlie sighed. "Grab that bugbear, the one you call Gigi. We'll start with her."

I was horrified to see Travis clap his hands in agreement. Sure, Gigi was being a jerk, but I didn't think her superior attitude and grammatical haughtiness were reason enough to kill her.

"Not just kill her, you uninspired nitwit," Charlie snarled. "There'll be torture with meat hooks, hanging her by her own entrails—you get the idea. It's much more involved than simply *killing* her."

Oh, poop.

I tried to find Allison and let her know what was going on so she could warn Gigi and get help, but every time I spotted her and tried to call out to her between classes, Charlie took over and made me foam at the mouth and bark like a dog. After two embarrassing incidents in the hallway, I gave up.

Travis and I went shopping that afternoon for supplies—Crisco, bungee cords, paper clips, and a dozen eggs. "Do I even want to know?" I muttered to Charlie.

No, he replied.

Travis had called his hockey buddies, who had agreed to meet him at the football field at dusk. Then he locked me in his trunk. "Sorry to do this, sweetie," he said, flashing those to-die-for dimples, "but I have to go pick up Gigi, and you'd cramp my style." I started to protest, but Charlie took over, and after a struggle for control of my body—during which I slapped my own face—Charlie made me climb meekly into the Civic's trunk. At least it was roomy.

Travis drove for a while, then stopped the car. A short time later, I heard slightly muffled voices.

"Really, Travis. It's supposedly, not supposably. You're lucky you're cute."

Yup. That was definitely Gigi.

More driving, then the car slowed. I felt us turn, and figured we were pulling into the entrance of the football stadium. Travis told Gigi to meet him at the goal post—he was going to get a blanket out of the trunk. She giggled and got out of the car.

Not so bright as you think, are you, Gigi? I thought.

See? She deserves to die, Charlie said.

Travis winked at me as he opened the trunk. I wanted to smack those dimples right off his face, but Charlie made me scramble out of the trunk, and we followed Travis across the grass. Other shadowy figures moved in from around the field. Great. The varsity hockey team was here in full force.

"Travis? What's she doing here?" Gigi pouted, spotting me. "I thought we were going to have some alone time?" *Oh, Gigi. You idiot*, I fumed, but Charlie kept me silent.

"Good news, Gigi. We've decided to make you our first sacrifice in Satan's plan to take over the world." Travis beamed, then grabbed Gigi by the hair, pulling her to him.

"Oh no you don't!" came a voice from behind me. I spun to see Allison, flanked on one side by Mike Tierney, he of the newly removed braces—and first-string left wing for the Tomahawks. He was carrying a large cooler. On Allison's other side stood a thin, shaky young man holding a cross and wearing a clerical collar. I recognized him as the junior pastor from our church. "Pastor Simon!" I said, relieved.

Travis turned to scowl at the pastor. Gigi took the opportunity to kick him right in the apple bag, and he let out a shrill gasp of shocked pain. The rest of the hockey team hesitated, a few letting out sympathetic groans as Travis doubled over.

"Now!" Allison shouted, and Mike stepped forward, dumping the contents of his cooler over my head. It burned like acid, and Charlie and I howled in unison.

"What the hell?" I yelped.

"Holy water. Go to it, Pastor—and hurry!"

The blistering agony of the holy water was unbearable. Charlie tried to break into a run, and although the lizard part of my brain wanted to flee too, I struggled to stop him. He was too strong, and started pumping my legs, but I couldn't let us get away—this demonic possession had to end, once and for all. I wanted my friends back; and as nice as it was to be a hottie, Travis Pullman was not turning out to be the perfect boyfriend I'd imagined him to be. If his was the kind of attention I'd be getting from now on, I could live without the fabulous hair and skin. I concentrated my efforts on one section of my body, and managed to wrangle control of my right foot away from Charlie. Using that, I tripped us. We fell flat on my face, then quickly rolled over. Pastor Simon loomed above us.

He quickly recited the "Our Father" in a solemn tone, waving his cross over me. He ended by chanting "The power of Christ compels you!" three times, then laid the crucifix on my chest. Charlie bellowed, letting loose such caterwauls as had never been heard this side of terra firma. I joined him, screeching as I felt my soul ripping apart. I was sure I was dying. I wanted my mom.

Then, in an instant, all was quiet. The boiling pain was gone. I curled into a ball and cried. Allison handed me a Kleenex.

"Sorry, Jules. But it had to be done."

"Thanks," I said, and meant it. "How did you know where we were?"

"Mike," she said, nodding at the burly left-winger, who was gazing at Allison like a puppy dog. "I told you he got his braces off. We've been dating for, like, two days now. You never listen to me." She frowned.

"But how did you know what to do? Pastor Simon? Have you done this before?"

"No," he admitted, and relieved his shaky knees by sitting down next to me. "But I watched the episode of Marlena's exorcism on *Days Of Our Lives* this week, and I took notes."

What? He'd just performed . . . a soap opera exorcism on me?

He sure did, Jules, Charlie cackled. *Now your friend there thinks I'm gone. And you won't have a chance to tell her the truth, because I think I'll be taking over from here. We can do the devil's work without anyone knowing what we're up to.*

Oh, poop.

DOWN THE CORRIDOR OF THE
FORGOTTEN MIND

It started slowly, Mariah losing things.

At first it was stuff she could chalk up to ordinary absentmindedness: searching for a folder only to find she'd been holding it the whole time, or discovering her glasses in the refrigerator and just then realizing she hadn't been wearing them. Had she forgotten she needed them to read? Missing her exit off the highway because her head was in the clouds. Little instances of lost time.

She chalked up these momentary lapses of reason to stress. Neil had come home last month with the announcement he'd been fired again—the eighth job he'd lost in their fifteen years of marriage—for telling politically incorrect jokes on the job. "It'll be fine, Mare-Bear. I'll find something else." She'd winced at the nickname—it was an endearment her father had called her, and in her heart, he was the *only* one who'd ever be allowed to use it, though he'd been dead . . . how long? A long time. Point was, there was a mortgage to pay, and car loans, and the burden of being both the primary wage-earner and the one cleaning the house, cooking meals, doing laundry, buying birthday gifts for aging in-laws and sending Christmas cards to cousins she'd never met and *someone* had to mow the lawn before the neighbors complained—it all fell on Mariah. She had the weight of the world on her shoulders, bearing down on her brain every waking moment. It was no wonder some things might've leaked out of her mind and escaped with the wind.

It was seeping into her typing, too. She caught herself several times reversing the letters in common words—thier instead of their, for instance, and she'd pause, backspacing to correct the error. That was odd. She was the grammar *queen*, couldn't even read mass-market paperbacks because she found the mistakes so irritating she'd switched to audiobooks a year ago—and figured it was a one-time thing. After all, she was the woman who'd turned off autocorrect in Word because the stupid program kept *introducing* errors.

Jared, her coworker and the man she'd been having an affair with the past nine months or so, bounced over to her desk one afternoon looking like a dog who'd just earned a *good boy!* for doing nothing more than not piddling on the carpet. He was waving a printout of the email she'd shot him no more than five minutes earlier.

"So you *are* capable of making mistakes!" he crowed triumphantly.

"I never said I wasn't." She'd started sleeping with the handsome pharmaceutical rep, ten years her junior, just to see if there was anything better out there than what she had now with Neil. Jared was funny and brooding and smart, and, from what she'd seen of his condo—he lived ten minutes away from the office, convenient for nooners—a slob, and the kind of man who would rather spend his money restoring an old Harley ("The same model Fonda rode in *Easy Rider!*" he'd said, beaming) than paying the electric bill ("I'll catch up on it next paycheck—c'mon, don't be a pill. Candlelight's *romantic.*"). He used paper plates because washing real ones was too much effort, and would Febreze jeans for one more wear instead of running a load of wash.

Jared had shown her that no, there wasn't anything much better out there. Such a shame—she'd *wanted* to fall in love with him. Still, the sex was fantastic.

"What are you going on about?" Her eyes narrowed at the email he was still waving like a trophy.

"You misspelled your own name! Wait—it *is* I-A-H, right?" A shadow of doubt crossed his lightly freckled face.

She snatched the paper from him and squinted—yup, there it was in print for all the world to see. She'd reversed the I and A, signing off as Maraih. *This is insane. I must be overtired.* She managed to laugh it off.

"Looking forward to the AMA conference next week?" Jared murmured. "I know I am." The two of them were traveling up to Portsmouth for the event, staying overnight at the Westin, which their employer was springing for. There was something sexy and dangerous about fooling around in a hotel on the company's dime.

"Can't wait," she said distractedly. She shooed him off and turned back to her computer screen. She had to reluctantly admit it was time to turn the autocorrect feature back on.

It took her a good twenty minutes to figure out how to do it, though.

Mariah kept losing the little things, and the pace at which they fell away sped up to a canter. She neglected to call her favorite uncle on his birthday, for which her cousin Gwen called to chew her out; an overdue notice from the cell phone company arrived—she'd forgotten to pay the bill. She sat in her car one morning for over five minutes in the rain, unable to wrap her mind around how to turn the windshield wipers on. She used *amorous* when she'd meant *arduous* during a fight with her husband, and found herself having to pretend to feel romantic after the slip-up defused the tension.

She thought she'd been covering admirably well, until Neil cornered her in the kitchen one day, running a hand through his neatly styled salt-and-ginger hair (*and guess whose paycheck sprang for that salon job*, she thought with a frown)."I'm worried about you. I think you should go to the doctor." And Neil *did* look worried—*probably because he can't have his meal ticket out of commission*, Mariah figured. She thought of Jared with a twinge of anger—when she'd scrambled to remember his name yesterday, his expression had reflected annoyance, not concern like this unsufferable moron.

That's not fair. For all his faults, Neil does love you. Out loud, she said, "I'm fine."

"Really?" He held a soggy sneaker. "You ran my Nikes through the dishwasher."

She blinked at the accusatory shoe. Had she? "I read an article saying that was the best way to clean them. You were *just* complaining how dirty they are." It was a lie. She'd read no such article and Neil had said no such thing.

Mercifully, he let it go.

"Your fly is down." Neil was by the front door, holding a to-go cup of coffee. She thanked him, zipped up her pants, and took the cup. He kissed her cheek. "See you tomorrow afternoon."

Was he going somewhere? Wait—he'd said he was starting a new job this week . . . doing what? Mariah searched the cobwebbed recesses of her mind and came up empty. She couldn't ask—that would prove she hadn't been listening. She'd been tuning him out for months, just for sanity's sake, and lo and behold, for the first time in ages, he'd imparted something important, instead of his usual stupid prattling about the weather or dead animals he'd spotted on the side of the road.

Well. She'd have the house to herself that night. That was something to look forward to.

At the office, the receptionist—*her name starts with T or H*—quirked an eyebrow when Mariah rushed in (she'd missed her exit *again*, darn it). "Why aren't you on your way to the Westin?"

The ADA conference—*no, AMA. Oh no!*

"Just have to get something from my desk." Mariah hurried toward her cubicle, grabbed a Post-It, pulled up her email, and started scribbling. She spun heel and took off again in seconds, offering Terry or Helen or whatever the heck her name was a half wave as she left.

She clambered into her car, pausing to swipe a sleeve at the sweat prickling her forehead, and looked at the Post-It where she'd scrawled the convention address. Her phone. There was something on her phone that could tell her how to get there, but when she unlocked her screen with her fingerprint—*thank god for that, if I had a gun to my head I still wouldn't be able to think of the password*—she couldn't think of the app's name that would get her there. She must've left her thumb on the home button too long, because the phone beeped at her—"How can I help you today?" a cheery computer lady asked—and she sputtered, "Get me directions to 12575 Industrial Drive?" A quick glance in the back seat told her she'd packed an overnight bag—when?—though she wouldn't bet money she'd remembered a toothbrush. "Starting route to 12575 Industrial Drive, Portsmouth," the computerized lady announced.

She found the conference center. And, thankfully, Jacob. *Jared. Darn it!*

The lectures were dry and tedious and the networking cocktail hour unbearable. She let Jared do the talking, swapping business cards and spouting on about their newest client—*some sleep aid. Ambivalent? Amababa? Whatever it is, maybe I should take it*—while Mariah sat on an uncomfortable stool, smile plastered on her face, and let her mind wander. She pictured her brain as a white-washed corridor, with doorways lining the hall, and she glided down the waxy-sheen floors in the goofy cow slippers her grandmother had given her one Christmas decades ago, when Mariah was maybe ten. She'd pause at a doorframe here and there, peering in at the wispy memories, seeing a face or breathing in a scent that was both familiar and unidentifiable.

I can see the cuckoo bird in the cuckoo tree. It was a line from something—a play?—but it was enough to snap Mariah back to the present. Where was Jamie? Her eyes sought him out, found him at the bar with a silver-haired man, both men smiling and showing impossibly white teeth. She stood. Her lover caught her glance, gave a slight nod, and within seconds, was by her side. "Want to turn in?"

Had they eaten? She wasn't sure. "We can order room service, you know . . . later," he said, answering her unasked question.

She let him guide her upstairs to his room.

After sex and a nap, she watched him get up, pull on his boxers, and answer the door. He rifled through her purse, pulling out several bills, and disappeared from her view, only to return moments later holding a platter. He set the tray on the bed and lifted the lids, displaying fettucine alfredo and sausage with peppers and onions, chest puffed out like he'd made it all himself. It did look good. She was pretty sure she liked Italian.

Her lover whose name she was certain started with a J skipped the napkins, using the back of his hand to nick the alfredo sauce off his chin and wipe it on the comforter. He chatted about the Orioles and Miguel Castro being recalled from Bowie. She thought of birds and Cuba and "Changes" and how this handsome man was a total slob, and didn't seem to know her at all—she gave not one fig about Cuba or birds or baseball. The pretty singer with the crazy mismatched eyes, him she thought she liked.

Still, the sex was fantastic. When they cuddled later, all urges temporarily sated, a tear escaped, trickling down her cheek.

This was the last time. She didn't know why, but she knew it to be true, and she thought she might miss this.

Mariah closed her eyes, pulling on her cow slippers to skid down the corridors of her mind like a child on roller skates.

She fell into a pattern: slide, skid, stop at a door, peek in. One room was filled with sand, soft waves rolling in the distance. Overhead, a gull cawed. She kicked off her slippers and stepped onto the warm grit, letting it sift between her toes. Mariah giggled, running toward the ocean, gasping when the brisk water engulfed her calves, numbing them. A school of bait fish darted by, glittering orange in the briny sea. She dunked a hand beneath the waves, letting the minnows glide over her palm; she lifted her fingers to her mouth. The salt tasted of her childhood. If she looked to her left, down the coastline, she was sure she'd see her father—gone now almost ten years—casting a line, tipping the brim of his fishing hat against the sun, waiting patiently for a bite. She turned, her eyes seeking out his familiar profile, but Papa Bear was nowhere to be found.

She needed to find another doorway. One to the old family bakery, where surely her father would be kneading dough, flour sprinkled over arms and pants and maybe a dab on the tip of his nose.

She brushed off her feet against her calves as best she could, then tucked them back into the cow slippers. How excited she'd been opening that gift—it was the Christmas of '83, she remembered now—and her grandmother's round porcelain face, puffed up from the prednisone, beamed as Mariah squealed in delight at the black-and-white-patterned slip-ons. The brain tumor had taken Grandma Beverly only three months later; how had Mariah possibly forgotten that? She skimmed on down the slick hallway, pausing at doors to look for Grandma, and Mama, and Papa Bear.

She finally spotted the opening to the back room to the bakery, where giant mixers churned, but there was no sign of her father. Another bore the old crabapple tree behind her uncle's house, the one she and her cousin Gwennie climbed as children, hoping to touch the sky. A third held her childhood bedroom, posters of David Bowie holding court over a bed littered with stuffed animals. She stopped here, scooping up her overall-donned cat, Clementine, squeezing her tight. Gone were the worn spots where Mariah had worried Clem's fur away: the cat's black eyes were shiny, her orange fuzz thick. Clementine made her feel young, and silly, and at peace again. As she hugged the goofy stuffed cat, the slouch that had curved Mariah's shoulders for so long straightened a bit as the weight of the world shucked away.

At the end of the corridor, another doorway. This one was darker, distorted somehow, and as Mariah skate-slid closer, Clem tucked under one arm, familiar tentacles of trepidation and despair hooked into her limbs. She wanted to stop . . . but there was something there. Something forgotten she had to see.

She stood by the entrance, peering into the abyss. Bright lights. White.

"I think she's waking up—nurse? Nurse!"

A figure hovered near the doorway, with salt-and-ginger hair and something simple about his face that made her think he probably had a nice disposition, but wasn't particularly smart. He wasn't unattractive, but not remarkable, either. He stood next to a second man, much handsomer, with big Kennedy teeth and dark freckles. How did these two know each other? They didn't look like they were related—to her, or each other. The only quality they seemed to share was that Mariah could picture herself being attracted to either one, or both, for very different reasons.

"Mariah?" the dreamboat asked.

"Don't you try to wake her, you bastard—that's *my* job," the other snapped, and Mariah smiled in surprise—she didn't think the simpleton had such fire in him. "Honey? Can you hear me?"

Through slitted eyes she studied both men. She suspected she *should* know who they were, but their names and faces were like water, and she couldn't get a solid grasp. She took a timid step forward, curious.

"See? I told you! She's waking up!"

Wiggling her toes, she found they were free of the Holstein slippers. Her heart sank. She wanted them *back*. And where did Clementine go? She considered throwing a temper tantrum to see if one of these schlubs would run out and fetch both slippers and doll for her. But the despair-tentacles had a stronger hold now, and through them the message was telegraphed that she was not allowed to behave that way. Grownups weren't ever to indulge in a good, soul-cleansing temper tantrum.

The handsomer man shrank back, as if acquiescing that yes, salt-and-ginger did have the official right to try and rouse Mariah. She studied the beta male. He sat down in a steel chair with no cushion—*that can't be comfortable*—and pulled out a vending-machine packet of pistachios. He cracked one open with his teeth, spat the shell into his hand, and dumped it on the ledge next to the window.

Disgusting. I hope I'm not in love with him.

The thought startled her, and she turned it over in her mind, examining it from all angles, as if there were a secret compartment in it she might spring open to discover this man's identity tucked inside. She pulled her focus back to salt-and-ginger, who was punching a red button at the end of a wire, as if this might bring her memories back. An alarm sounded; she thought it was distant at first, but the vibrations in her eardrum told her it was right near her head.

"Mariah? Sweetie? It's me. Honey? Squeeze my hand if you can hear me."

Sluggish synapses fired from brain to hand, and she felt this man's cool touch in her palm. She didn't like it. She wanted Clementine back.

A pert young woman in blue scrubs and a ponytail swam into view. "Step aside, please. Mrs. Kaplan? Mariah? I'm just going to check your pupils, okay?" A pinpoint of blinding light. "Reactive. That's great news."

"So she *is* waking up," salt-and-ginger said, a question more than a statement. "What does this mean? How soon can she go back to work?"

The question set off alarm bells in Mariah, louder than the beeping in the room. A word popped to mind, with creepy-crawly legs and a sucker-shaped mouth: *parasite.*

Shrinking back, she tried to retreat to her corridor, but when she turned, she found only haze. *No!*

"Mariah? Come on now, baby. It's me. I love you. *Please* wake up." Salt-and-ginger sounded sincere, but the word *parasite* still skittered in the corners of the room, looking for a host to latch onto.

From the vapor of the fading corridor, a different voice: softer, weaker, questioning, but also gravid with hope: "Mare-Bear?"

"Papa Bear!" She wrenched her mind free from the white staleness of the hospital bed, from what a small voice told her was likely sanity. She didn't care—if madness was where her father and happiness lay, she'd take it willingly and without regret. She threw herself through the doorway, half-expecting to fall into a cloud of endless smoke but not caring. The warm fleece of her cow slippers enveloped her feet as she landed, her heel sliding on the polished linoleum. And there, in the distance, her father: the yeasty scent of fresh-baked loaves tickled her nose across the expanse of the hallway.

She hesitated, glancing over at the doorway she'd just escaped through. Spotted what she was looking for. And pulled on the thick iron door with all her strength, feeling a burning ache in her arms as she tugged, waiting only until she heard the click of the heavy lock engage before whirling back to skate-slide her way to her father.

BUCKET LIST

"That leaves just one last item," Annamarie said, neatly crossing *eat a deep-fried pickle* off her bucket list. Her gray, paper-thin skin looked resplendent against the bleached white sheets of the hospice bed. She wasn't wearing a wig this bright morning, and I marveled yet again at the perfect symmetry of her skull: not one dent or mismatched bump graced her sleek dome.

I'd fallen in love with her hard, from the first moment I met her at a used book sale. We'd both reached for the same tattered copy of Ray Bradbury's *The Martian Chronicles*, and wound up spending the afternoon at Starbucks, discussing everything from eighties music to what kind of cretin, exactly, would ever give up a classic Bradbury to a book sale. Annamarie had been my whole world ever since. Five years after that first meeting, the diagnosis came: lung cancer, the irony of which was not lost on either of us. Annamarie had never so much as taken one puff of a cigarette in her entire forty-six years of life.

"Do you think it was the joint I smoked that time in college?" she asked, her terrified eyes brimming with tears of regret.

"No." I took her in my arms. "I think it's just rotten luck."

Once we were able to wrap our minds around the very worst of it—*four months, six at best*, the doctor had proclaimed solemnly, even after going through chemo and radiation as life-prolonging measures—Annamarie made up her mind to face her demise head-on. "I'm making a bucket list," she announced, and we'd spent the past twelve weeks crossing off each item, one by one.

At the start, it was easy: we visited the Poe statue in Boston and snapped funny-faced selfies, ate shawarma in Buffalo, went spelunking in Howe Caverns. We booked an impromptu three-day trip to the West Coast to see Disneyland and Grauman's Chinese Theatre. Before catching our flight home, we stopped off at Westwood Village Memorial Park to pay our respects graveside to Mr. Bradbury. It was the trip of a lifetime. It would have to be.

As she got sicker, the bucket list got harder: we had to reschedule our cruise around Martha's Vineyard twice because of bad reactions to the chemotherapy. When we finally did go—Annamarie was in a wheelchair at that point, unable to get enough oxygen in her mutinous lungs to stand and walk on her own—she wound up getting seasick. "There was no way getting around it," she announced. "I was going to puke on this trip one way or the other."

I was both relieved and terrified that we'd made it to the end of the list. "What's left?" I asked, sliding into bed next to her. "Skydiving? Meeting Denzel?"

"Seeing Queen live in concert."

"Are they even touring right now?" My heart squeezed out a painful off-beat. I couldn't disappoint her now, so close to the end . . .

She sighed, letting the list fall from hand to lap, closing her eyes. "If they're not, it's just as well. I always said I could die happy if I just saw Queen in concert. But I always kind've worried if I *did* see them, that would be it: I'd drop dead right then." Her eyes flew open, brighter: "But, of course, I was talking about Freddie Mercury's Queen. Maybe since it won't be him"—a smile tugged up her gaunt cheekbones—"It'll be the opposite. A miracle. Adam Lambert's voice might very well cure me!"

When you're facing something like the big C, and the worst possible outcome, you're willing to grasp onto anything. I thumbed up Queen's tour schedule and nearly whooped with victory: "They're playing the casino on Sunday. Sunday! I'm calling right now." Without so much as even checking to make sure this worked for Annamarie, I was already on hold with Ticketmaster.

I'll say this for Mohegan Sun: they're really something else with customer service when it comes to fulfilling a dying woman's last wish. Once I called ahead and explained the situation to the concierge, they pulled out all the stops. Valet parking. Complimentary drinks all night long. A free suite for the evening at the Sky Tower. Front row seats. For a bucket list wish item, Annamarie had saved the best for last.

She was weak that day, but excited: two rosy spots blushed high on her cheeks through her ashen pallor. She clapped when I rolled her wheelchair down the floor, not stopping until we were front and center of the stage. She actually *clapped*. It was a show of strength I hadn't seen from her in over a week. A delicate, birdlike hand went to the blue-paisley scarf on her head—it matched her cobalt eyes perfectly—and she pursed her lips at me, as if blowing a kiss.

I'd been worried about the weather—the humidity was a bear, even for those of us in the best of health—and the exposure to all the germs that surely hung in the casino air, what with all the people, from all over the country, the world, really, and she'd been so fragile lately, so worn out . . . *worth it*, my heart sang at that air-blown kiss. *Worth it, worth it, worth it.*

The lights dimmed, the smoke rose, and then the unmistakable opening beats of "We Will Rock You" thrummed through our very bones. Out from the mist onstage stepped a young man, eyeliner thick, hair and shirt the same plummy red, ordering us loudly, almost angrily, to make a big noise. I relaxed. *Hooted*, even, possibly for the first time in my five decades of life. Sang along to the chorus, pretending I was on a regular date, with my perfectly healthy wife, just a normal couple on a normal night and we were whole.

A feather-soft grip on my forearm. "Honey, do you see him? Oh, I don't believe it! Do you see?"

I glanced up at the stage again, at the young, whip-thin . . . *boy*, really, wearing an admittedly ridiculous crown atop his head, sounding not very much like the Queen we'd grown up with, but giving it a hell of a go just the same. "I see. Don't get your hopes up. I'm pretty sure he's—"

And then I saw. The boy's chest seemed to grow broader, his chin squarer. His struts across the stage were less angry, more cocky: and above the lip, the unmistakable shadow of a

Chevron mustache.

"Freddie." I barely heard her breathy whisper. And in less time than it took for Mercury to morph back into Lambert, my beloved, beautiful Annamarie was gone.

EARLY EVENING AT LEECH LAKE

Dawn was about to lie to her mother. It wasn't the first time. "Is it okay if I stay over Ashley's tonight?"

"I don't see why not. What do you girls have planned?"

"Nothing special," Dawn said, then winced. *Nothing special* sounded like a lie, a typical *We're not up to anything, I promise* type of answer. "She wants to rent a movie and hang out. She reserved *Poltergeist* at Blockbuster, so we figured we'd order pizza and watch that." Perfect. The more details in the lie, the more believable it sounded.

"*Poltergeist*? Isn't that supposed to be scary?"

Darn straight it was. They'd actually rented it *last* weekend, and Dawn was certain she'd now be terrified of stuffed clowns for the rest of her life. Possibly closets, too. But she played it cool, flipping her curly brown hair back as if the comment were a fly to be brushed off. "Come on, Mom. We're *seventeen*."

Her mother smiled. "Of course. All grown up—that's fine. But don't wake me up if you start having nightmares."

"Thanks, Mom." She gave her mother a quick kiss on the cheek and bounded upstairs to retrieve her already-packed duffel bag.

"Your mom buy it?" Ashley said, throwing her overnight bag in the back of Dawn's Jeep. Dawn nodded. "Mine too. Let's go."

The girls were headed to Leech Lake to spend the night at the campground with Ashley's boyfriend, Kevin, and his best friend, Bradley. When they were younger, Dawn couldn't stand Bradley—she'd developed her 32Ds early, and the freckle-faced redhead had delighted in snapping her bra all throughout fifth grade. But lately, his shoulders had broadened, his hair had deepened from copper to auburn, and she could hardly see his freckles under his golden tan. Dawn was excited he'd agreed to the overnight.

They were meeting the boys at the lake. On the way, the girls stopped at a Wawa's for cookies, candy, pre-made sandwiches, and chips and dip. The guys were in charge of beer and sleeping bags. Dawn and Ashley just had to supply the food.

"You kids having a party?" the Wawa's clerk asked as he punched prices into the register.

"We're heading to the lake for the night," Ashley said, eyeing the bug sprays on the counter. She plucked one out of the display and tossed it next to a bag of Skittles.

"I wouldn't go there if I were you." The clerk gave the girls a stern look over a pair of wire-rimmed glasses. "Bad things happen out at the lake."

Dawn laughed nervously. "What? There a homicidal maniac in a hockey mask running around out there?"

The man shook his head slowly. "Worse. The bacteria levels in the lake water have been testing real high this summer. You could get sick. Plus, folks around here have a tendency to walk their dogs around the campground. And they don't"—he punctuated the word with a fist on the counter—"pick up"—another thump—"their poop! There's free doggy dookie bags all over the goll-dern place, but they're too lazy to clean up after Fido. That's just lazy pet ownership!"

Ashley shot a look of *clearly a sore spot* to Dawn. "Well—uh—we don't have any dogs. I mean, my mom has a Yorkie, but we keep her in the house. Or back yard. She's not with us."

"I'm just warning you kids. Don't go swimming in the lake." He handed them their bags. "And watch where you step!"

"Thank you," Dawn mumbled.

"And watch out for snapping turtles!" the clerk added. The bell jingled over the door as they made their exit.

"What a freak!" Ashley said with a laugh. "Think he's stepped in dog doo one too many times?"

"I'd say so." Dawn turned the ignition key, and they headed off to meet their dates.

"I hate to sound rude, but what's he doing here?" Dawn whispered to Ashley as they pulled up next to Kevin's Scout. Ashley's boyfriend was leaning up against his car, Bradley and

Harry "Hacksaw" Hackman next to him. "I thought it was just supposed to be the four of us."

"I thought so too." Ashley scowled. "I hate that guy. Hacksaw's the one who put a dead rat in my locker freshman year. I mean, it was rubber, but still." She slid off the front seat, flouncing over to Kevin and wrapping her arms around his neck. Kevin's hands went right to her butt, where he gave her a playful drumroll on the cheeks. "Hi, babe."

"Hi," she cooed. "What's with the fifth wheel?" Ashley jerked her chin toward Hacksaw.

"We had to bring him. His brother's the one who bought the Pabst."

"Nice to see you too," Hacksaw said loudly.

Ashley rolled her eyes, returning to the Jeep. "You guys want to help us with our bags?"

"Nope," Hacksaw said, but Kevin and Bradley trailed her to the car.

"This place sucks," Bradley said, scraping dog doo off the bottom of his left sneaker. It was the most he'd said in the hour since they'd arrived. Ashley nudged Dawn with her elbow.

Dawn cleared her throat. She grabbed a Pabst from the cooler, popped the top of the can, and sauntered over to Bradley. "Here. Maybe this'll help."

He gave her a sour look. "I don't drink."

"Of course you don't," Dawn murmured. "Um . . . neither do I, really." She made to tip out the contents of the can on the ground.

"Hey, hey, hey! That's alcohol abuse!" Hacksaw snatched the can out of Dawn's grip, so that he now had one in each hand. He looked down, then held the beers up, letting out a whoop. "Double-fisted, dude!"

Kevin held up his beer, clinking against both of Hacksaw's in a salute.

"This place sucks," Dawn said.

"Kevin and I are going to take a walk in the woods," Ashley said. "Think you'll be all right?"

Dawn glanced over at Bradley, who was sitting on a log, arms crossed over his stomach, eyes closed. Her gaze shifted to Hacksaw, who was rolling his empty Pabst cans up in his long, shaggy blond hair, looking not unlike a grandmother at a beauty salon. "I guess?" she replied.

"Great. Thanks."

Once the couple was gone, Dawn tried again with Bradley. She ambled over to his log and sat down next to him. She held out the open bag of Skittles. "Want some?"

"God, no," Bradley said. "The red dye in those things causes cancer, you know."

She hesitated, a red Skittle pinched between two fingers, then dropped it back in the bag and set the whole thing aside. After a minute of silence, she tried again, nudging his foot with her toe. "What'cha thinking about?"

"How this was a stupid idea. The only reason why I came is 'cause Kevin promised to get me a date with Cara McAdams if I did."

Dawn blinked at him, then reached for the bag of candy again, fishing out all the red ones and chewing them slowly, deliberately, so Bradley would see. Damn that Ashley! *Bradley is super into you,* her best friend had lied. This whole thing had been a setup so Ashley could spend the night hooking up with Kevin.

"Hey, don't bogart the Skittles. Give some here," Hacksaw said. He'd found a length of PVC pipe somewhere in the brush nearby, and held it to his lips. "Pour some down the tube and I'll catch 'em in my mouth."

Dawn sighed, then stood. At least Hacksaw didn't seem to be miserable in her company. She moved to sit on the ground next to him, stopping at the cooler first to grab a beer, then pouring a handful of candies down the pipe. Hacksaw choked, then giggled. He gestured with the PVC. "You wanna try?"

She took him in: his stained Bart Simpson T-shirt advising her to not have a cow; his lanky, tanned legs sprawled in the dirt in front of him; his Pabst-can hair rollers. "What the hell." She held out her hand for the pipe. Hacksaw squealed in delight and grabbed a handful of candies.

An hour later, Dawn was pleasantly buzzed from the beer. She and Hacksaw were giggling and whispering conspiratorially, occasionally stealing glances at Bradley. "He snapped the bra holding *those* wonders up?" Hacksaw asked, eyeing the front of her tank top. "How'd he even wedge a finger in the strap to do it?"

Bradley stood abruptly, brushing off his jeans. "I'm gonna go look for Kevin and Ash. They've been gone a while."

"I'm not sure they want to be found," Dawn said. Was she slurring?

"Let him go," Hacksaw cut in. "Gives *us* some time to get to know each other better." He nudged her arm with his elbow.

Bradley walked with purpose toward the path down which Kevin and Ashley had disappeared earlier. A few seconds later, they heard: "C'mon now! Why can't people clean *up* after their pets?" Dawn and Hacksaw dissolved in another fit of laughter.

Once Bradley's footsteps had disappeared, Hacksaw looked at her earnestly. *Oh, wow. Is he going to kiss me?* Dawn felt sobriety rush over her like a cold shower. Did she even want to hook up with Hacksaw? He was funny enough, but he had a reputation at school of being sort of a slacker. But . . . he *was* cute, especially after she'd had two beers. She decided to let him.

"Tell me honestly," he said, gazing deep into her eyes. "Did the rollers work?" He tugged the beer cans out of his hair. "I've always kinda wanted naturally wavy hair. How do I look?"

His hair hung in limp waves, resembling seaweed. Dawn smiled. "Sure it did."

He leaned in closer, close enough for her to catch a whiff of sour beer in his hair. "I think you might be lying."

"Would I—" but he cut her off with a kiss before she could finish.

She closed her eyes. *Well, this is . . . this is . . .*

. . . this is gross. Hacksaw was a terrible kisser. Too much tongue, and he slobbered spit down her chin. She pulled back, breaking the lip lock, when the crashing of trees and underbrush made her freeze.

Something *big* was coming, and from the sounds of it, it was heading right for them.

"Wow," Hacksaw said drunkenly. "I think I felt the earth move with that kiss." He scooted closer, lips pursed as if to Hoover her in again.

"That wasn't us, you dolt! Don't you hear that?"

It sounded like an elephant was barreling through the woods. Dawn shoved Hacksaw away as she stood, and he scrambled to stand up beside her. "What do you think it is?" she whispered. He shrugged, then put a hand on her tank top, over her left breast.

"Are you kidding me right now?" She slapped his hand off. "Something's coming! Should we run?"

Before Hacksaw could answer, Bradley broke out from the tree line. He was running sort of lopsidedly, and holding something against his body, pinned there with his right arm. When he staggered closer to them, Dawn realized the thing he was holding tightly between right arm and torso was his *left* arm. It had been severed close to the shoulder, a ragged stump of flesh and bone poking accusingly in her direction.

"T-t-" he gasped.

"What is it? Spit it out, man!" Hacksaw said, his voice rising. He sniffed. "Dude. Did you step in dog shit or something?"

"T-t-*turtle*! Run!"

As soon as Bradley got the word out, a large, lumbering silhouette waddled alarmingly quickly out of the trees. A giant shell the size of a two-car garage and covered in mud topped four enormous scaled feet, which ended in claws resembling white railroad spikes. Its head and face peaked in a glossy, razorlike beak the width of a truck. Dawn guessed this was the source of Bradley's recent amputation. Lidded eyes the size of dinner plates, dappled with black dots in the pattern of a cross, skimmed the campsite before settling on the three teens.

"Is that a dinosaur?" Hacksaw asked.

"Snapping turtle," Dawn said, almost reverently. The giant reptile was both breathtaking and the stuff of nightmares, in one horrible, beautiful package.

"Run!" Bradley said again, and began his flailing stagger-jog again, toward the path leading to the parking lot.

The turtle's head snapped toward Bradley, the skin under its beak swaying like the turkey wattle of an old woman. It studied its escaping prey for only a few seconds before returning its gaze to Dawn and Hacksaw.

Is it smiling? Dawn thought absurdly, then shook her head. It was a trick of the beak, nothing more.

Hacksaw seemed unable to grasp the situation. "It can't be a snapper," he said, even as the monster took a step closer, its claws spayed grotesquely against the dirt. "They don't get that big."

Dawn scanned the campsite, looking for something she could use as a weapon. "You go ahead and argue with it." She spotted the PVC pipe. Better than nothing. She squatted, scooped it up, and readied it like a baseball player gearing up to hit a home run.

"Good thinking," Hacksaw said. "If we can get it to shotgun Skittles, it'll be too busy chewing to attack, and we can make our escape."

"You're an idiot," Dawn said. Then she gave him a shove toward the snapping turtle.

The beast's neck stretched impossibly long and its jaws opened wide, revealing a pale pink mouth. In a blink its beak clamped shut.

Hacksaw's head was gone. His body took one more step forward, as if still trying to correct itself from Dawn's push, before tumbling to the ground.

The giant turtle swallowed, then took a fleshy bite out of Hacksaw's torso. It tossed its head back to gulp down the meat, then dipped in again.

Now! Dawn rushed forward, PVC pipe held in front of her like a ramming rod. Her aim was true, and she jammed the pipe into the reptile's right nostril, sinking it in at least two feet. She didn't wait to see if the snapping turtle was dead or only wounded. She whirled toward the path down which Bradley had fled, and ran until her calf muscles burned and her Jeep was in sight.

Bradley was slumped next to Kevin's Scout, his severed arm on the ground beside him. Dawn kicked him. "You dead?"

"Ow, stop! Just resting!" He retrieved his arm. "What happened?"

Dawn couldn't speak. She climbed into the Jeep, turning the key.

The motor wouldn't turn over.

"No! No, no, no!" She slammed her hands on the steering wheel.

"Don't panic. Give it a minute; you probably flooded the engine."

She didn't appreciate Bradley's patronizing tone. She turned to look at him. "Shut up. You're lucky I even let you into my car, the way you smell. What'd you do, *roll* in the dog poo?"

"Excuse me," he said, holding up his left arm and shaking it at her. "I got my arm bitten off, and you're worried about your precious *floor mats* smelling?"

Dawn screamed.

The snapping turtle was weaving its way toward the Jeep, PVC pipe jutting angrily from its nostril. It clambered across the lot, its soulless eyes laser-focused on Dawn and Bradley.

"Drive!" Bradley shrieked.

Dawn held her breath as she jiggled the key in the ignition, then tried turning it over again.

The engine roared to life. Dawn threw the car in reverse, bringing them within inches of the monster's whetted beak, then put it in drive, tires squealing. In the rearview mirror, Dawn could see the snapping turtle striking where the vehicle had just been, jaws cracking shut on nothing but air.

Dawn and Bradley drove without speaking for a few minutes, Bradley hunching over to study the side mirror as they fled. After a few minutes, Dawn cleared her throat. "Ashley? Kevin?"

Bradley shook his head. "I don't think they made it."

Dawn let up on the gas. "But you don't know for sure?"

"I'm not about to volunteer to go back and check, are you?"

"You know, you've got a real attitude. I can't believe I had a crush on you."

Bradley barked a short, mean laugh. "Seriously? Not a chance. You'll always be that dumpy nerd with the bad training bra in Mrs. Bennett's fifth grade class. No thanks. You're not my type."

Dawn debated leaving him on the side of the road and letting him walk to a hospital. But then she remembered something he'd said earlier, and smiled.

He cocked an eyebrow. "What're you grinning about, Dumpy?"

"Cara McAdams. You know she's gay, right?"

"Shut up. She is not."

"She's been with Erika Peters since we were sophomores. Wow, you're dumb."

"I hate you, Dumpy."

"I'm sorry the turtle didn't swallow your arm, Stumpy."

They fell into silence again. Dawn didn't mind; she had other problems besides her crush turning out to be a grade-A turdblossom. She didn't know *what* she was going to tell her mother when she got home.

WINTER OF MY DISCONTENT

When Milt told me he'd been hired by James Reed to drive oxen across the Wasatch Mountains, I'd felt all the excitement and naiveté that only the newly married, filled with rosy pipe dreams of the future, can understand.

"The party? You've been hired on to go to California?" The words came out in a breathless rush.

"I have," Milt said, sweeping me up in a spin and planting a wet kiss on my cheek. "No more potato pancakes and moldy bread for us. We're going to California!"

My head filled with images of fine Sunday dresses and polished black boots. We'd heard the whispers, the glinting awe that shimmered in the voices of those who spoke of California. Those words sparkled with flecks of gold.

"Oh, Milt, really?"

"Really. Pack your bags. We're officially signed on with the Donner-Reed party!"

Shivering under this worn tarp now, it's hard to recapture that feeling of excitement the next days held. Packing our canvas bags with frocks appropriate for summer and fall, many which have since been shredded for bandages when their loose weaves proved too thin to offer any protection against the biting snow, is but a distant memory. And what I wouldn't give for a bite of moldy bread!

I blame Lanford Hastings for our plight. The arrogant pismire sent word early on to our party that the Mexicans were acting up along the Fort Hall Trail, and convinced the impulsive James Reed to take leave of his senses and follow a new path, one Lanford had loftily named the Hastings Cutoff. Up until this point, our delays had been minor—we had to sit tight for but a day due to a rising river, and the rains made things muddy, but otherwise, the journey had been pleasant. Eleanor Eddy and I became fast friends as we darned socks by the fire each night, still dreaming of streets paved with gold. So full of hope. So stupid.

Any fool could see just by looking at it that Hastings Cutoff was a poor choice. The ice-capped mountains stabbed violently at the sky, hiding cliffs and canyons and long stretches of plains between, all offering no easy travel. But James Reed and William Eddy were convinced by Hastings' smooth serpent tongue that we could shave off the days lost to rain by taking his pass, and avoid Mexican bullets to boot. We weren't but a day on the trail, our horses putting down tenuous hooves among the sharp rocks, when a large boulder, bigger than the little shack Milt and I'd left in Springfield, blocked our way. Milt and George Donner scouted around it, quickly returning with bad news: we'd not be passing by unless the behemoth stone was moved.

It was hot work, even just watching the men yoke the oxen and tie ropes. Eleanor and I observed their efforts from under an oak bare of leaves, the sun scorching us until we were soggy as the steamed oysters we'd heard were so popular in San Diego. By the time the boulder had begrudgingly trundled to the left, giving up only so many inches to allow us to pass single file, we had to pitch tents for the night.

As sweltering as the days were, the night temperatures were determined to turn our beads of sweat to frostbite. Milt was so worn out from the day's toils he turned away from me when I reached for him, the first time he'd done so since we'd been wed two months prior. I cupped my elbows, shivering, waiting for those first embers of resentment to burn high enough to offer me warmth.

The next days, we fared no better. The inclines were so steep no sane man would've dared try to forge his way, but we had no choice. Wagon wheels were locked to avoid rolling back; Tamsen Donner sprained her ankle trying to lead her gelding through a particularly rock-ribbed path. Luke Halloran, whose symptoms of consumption had become quite apparent early on the trip, had to be shuttled from wagon to wagon, where he often passed out from the pain of the jarring terrain. The sunbeams carving into our men's backs during the days did nothing to alleviate the frosty nights, and tempers soon grew short.

"Another note from Hastings!" Eleanor announced, six days into our climb. Hastings had left two posts already, affixed to trees along the cutoff with crudely carved wooden nails.

"I hope he's written to admit his terrible mistake, and to inform William of what a fool he is," I muttered. I left it open to Eleanor's interpretation whether it was Hastings or her husband I was naming the fool.

"As I recall, your husband was just as eager to cross the cutoff as the other men," Eleanor chided. She was smiling, but the expression didn't quite reach her eyes.

"Well, marry in haste, repent in leisure. I'm starting to see the truth in that," I admitted.

"Oh, hush. You don't mean that. It's the heat blistering your senses."

I nodded. But when Milt came up behind us to peck my cheek and snatch up the latest word from Hastings, I wiped away his kiss with my sleeve as he turned away.

The squall took us by surprise one week in.

"Snow? In August? Impossible!" Milt said, though the flakes pelting the tarp told a different story. We huddled around a makeshift fire with some of the Reeds and with Charles, a herdsman like Milt.

"We should collect some snow and melt it down to shore up our water," Charles suggested. "We're about out, and"—his voice dropped—"you didn't hear it from me, but I believe the McCutcheons have stopped providing drink to poor Halloran."

"He'd be better off if he just gave up the ghost," I whispered, and there was more than one murmur of agreement.

"We need to feed this fire," Eleanor said, and glanced up, as if dazed at the thought. "What can we use for kindling?"

"Here. These old posts can go," Milt said, and pulled the worn missives from Hastings and Edwin Bryant, a writer who was but days ahead of us on the trail and had occasionally sent word back again of what we could expect on the path. Milt hadn't shared much of Bryant's letters, except to announce when water or game were plentiful ahead. Milt tossed the mail on the fire, where the flames caught the edges and blackened them to a curl in a blink. I squinted at the looped curves of Bryant's neat missives. I could just make out two words before the fire licked up the last of the paper:

Turn back.

The next word from Hastings advised us to stay put until he could backtrack and guide us through the next leg of our trek.

"Well, that's a fine how-do-you-do," I grumbled. The snow had melted in the day's heat, leaving gummy mud in its wake. We were moving perilously slow, and my mare, Windy, was having a hard time negotiating the sludge. "Remind me again why we didn't just stay on the California Trail?"

"Don't be such a sourpuss," Eleanor said. "It'll all work out. You'll see." But the usual sunniness was lacking in her tone. Her brows were knit tight, and my stomach sank when I realized Eleanor, she of unflagging faith and optimism, was worried.

Some of our men rode ahead to meet Hastings, who provided little more than a crudely drawn map showing a spiderweb of paths, before riding away again. We pressed on, but little was said as we fought mud, brush, and boulders. Several oxen were lost when the herdsmen drove them ahead to forge a path, only to drive them right off a canyon cliff.

"This is impossible!" I lamented.

"We can't turn back now," Milt said. I heard regret in his words.

We were a day's journey in across a dry, grassless plain when a party of twenty or so met up with us. The Graves had some stores—jerky, flour, and sugar—and more importantly, water, which we'd found ourselves dangerously short of before nightfall. We welcomed them heartily. The new faces and stories invigorated our little group of misery, and even the icy winds that night could not cut into the laughter that filled our camp for the first time in weeks.

The merriment did not last long. At the far end of the salt plain, we found scrub, no water, and no game. "We'll just press on," Milt said. He looked weary and—how much older was he now? The journey so far had aged him to the point where he no longer looked like my peer, but my father's. I was trapped: ensnared with an old man, in wild terrain, with only hunger and wretchedness to look forward to. We'd been perfectly happy and young, and knew nothing of frostbite or hunger, back in our dusty, dirt-floor shack in Springfield. How I missed the warm comfort of those clapboard walls and the bubbling of laundry in the kettle over the fire! We were tired, chilled to the bone, stomachs never ceasing to bark for attention, because of *him.* The salty air held my tongue still, but my heart knew what I could deny no longer: I'd made a poor choice in marrying Milt Elliott.

Luke Halloran died the next morning. "He was but skin and bones," Eleanor whispered. "'Twasn't the consumption that got him. I think he starved to death, and we're all to blame."

"Don't start now, Eleanor." I stomped my boot. "We're all hungry, and down to the barest of provisions! Why should a man who's been nothing but a burden since we set out get a share of bread that would be better served to a man who can clear rocks and branches from our path? His death is a blessing."

Eleanor blinked at me with watery eyes, touched her shoulders and forehead in the sign of the cross, and turned from me. It was the last conversation we had for the duration of the trip. I was now utterly alone, save for a husband whose mere touch made me shudder.

Then the snow *really* came.

It started without note; we were pressing through the Wasatch Mountains, determined to reach Sutter's Fort and salvation. It had been several days since Charles had shot, skinned, and shared the last antelope, and I'm sure we all had one thought occupying our minds: food. We had little, and we would surely die if we did not happen upon more quickly. What was left of the oxen—the ones that hadn't died on the route, or run off in crazed, starving delirium—were thin, exhausted, and covered in sores. Dreams of buffalo steak and dough biscuits clouded our eyes to the blizzard that formed around us.

Windy's stride broke suddenly. She let out a pained neigh and I found myself flying through the air, landing with a stinging thud on solid, snow-blanketed ground.

"Lenora!" Franklin Graves had seen my spill, and pulled his wagon up sharp. "Someone ride ahead and get Milt!"

"I'm okay," I called out, once I'd shaken off my surprise. This wasn't entirely true—there was a shrill complaint from my lower back when I sat up, but I was more concerned for my mare. "Check Windy. I don't know what caused her to throw me so!" I peered over to see if I could catch sight of my horse. In response, the snowfall doubled its efforts. Through the sheet of white, I could just make out Windy, who was struggling to get her feet under her, and failing.

Milt was at my side in moments, his burlap-gloved hand reaching down to help me up. "Windy," I said, the word a question.

"Looks like she caught a hole in the snow and turned her leg." He shook his head, pulling me close to him. It was meant to be a gesture of comfort, I'm sure, but I stiffened. "I'm sorry, Lenora. We'll have to put her down."

"No!" I slapped his chapped cheek. "She'll be okay. Probably just a twist. She'll recover in no time, you'll see." I wrested myself from his grasp and waded through the snow to get closer to my fallen girl. She was still struggling, her eyes wild, her sides heaving in deep breaths. Franklin put out an arm to keep me at a distance, and from there, I watched. Her front left leg was madly bent; my very soul went cold at the sight. Milt was right: there was no saving her. I turned away, the tears icing to my lashes before they could fall.

"We can camp here for the night," Charles called from his perch atop a handsome black steed. The wagons circled, to the right of where Windy still thrashed, and men began climbing down to lock wheels.

Milt was at my elbow again. "Go with Tamsen. Get warm. You don't need to be any part of this." He steered me toward the Donner wagon, and Tamsen opened her arms to beckon me.

"Part of what?" I murmured. The snow had my brain disoriented. Tamsen guided me up, inside her wagon, where blankets and company awaited. Then I heard the shot. "No!" I cried again.

"At least we'll eat tonight," I heard George Donner say outside the tent, but my grief, mercifully, did not allow me to comprehend the gruesome intent behind those words.

The meaty broth Tamsen roused me to eat in the middle of the night was delightful.

The blizzard was relentless, slowing us to a crawl. Mutterings among our party spoke of squatting down to wait out the winter.

"But that's impossible," I told Milt when he explained that to continue would be certain death. "We have, what? Twenty head left of oxen? Ten bags of flour? There are at least seventy of us. How will we eat?" We'd long since given up on the idea that we'd arrive in California with any sort of herd for the Donners and Reeds to sell at market; the Hastings Cutoff had done just that, cutting steers from our herd with its cliffs, caverns, and famine. "How long are we talking? A week? A month?"

"Until the snow stops," Milt said with a defeated shrug.

"So you don't know."

"I'm trying to keep us *alive*, woman."

I did not appreciate his tone.

We set up ramshackle tents and a couple of crude cabins right where we sat, near Truckee Lake. At least we would not want for water, with walls of it frozen all around us, but this was little comfort. Our stores of flour and beef were all but gone, the oxen and horses long slaughtered and et. We were cold, dirty, covered in lice, and starving.

The dogs were the first to go—just a few mutts in camp, six or so. The children put up a fuss, but 'twas George Murphy who first announced that we needed to think of them not as pets, but nourishment. He and Charles killed the first, skinning it, stripping it of meat, and parceling out the meager rations to each family.

"What will you do with those parts?" I asked, pointing to the skin, tail, and ears.

"Bury them, I suppose," George said.

"Oh, no, you won't," I said, pulling off my threadbare sweater to gather the extra bits and drag them back to our tent. The tail and ears were boiled down to a broth, and I eventually reduced the skin to a ghastly, foul-odored sludge that made Milt gag.

I did not care. I had to eat.

The feeling never left. I'd wake up, and before my eyes were fully open the cavernous ache of my empty stomach would throb. Many a morning I contemplated not even stirring from my nest of thin blankets and clothes; what was the point? But hunger would spur me to rise, and I'd wrap up as tightly as I could, stoke the fire, and venture outside to see if there was something—anything—to scavenge.

The frozen lake offered up no fish, and the game was wiser than we, having long since retreated to lower grounds to survive the winter. My morning hunts yielded little more than twigs and grass, brown and frozen beneath the snow. One morning, while digging at the icy tundra, I dislodged what I first took to be a date-sized, yellowed rock, but the shape was too even. I squinted, and my heart leapt. What I held was a bone—probably a vertebrae from some long-dead deer, and it was blanched bare of all meat, but that dark, porous substance in the center—could that be marrow?

I jerked my head at the cough above me. There stood Eleanor, ashen and stick-thin, peering over my shoulder. I pocketed the bone in my brassiere as if secreting away a steak. There was hardly enough marrow in the bone for one; I'd have to boil it when Milt was away from the tent. Surely Eleanor didn't think this bounty was for her, too . . . ?

Her glare was as piercing as the frigid wind, but she said nothing, moving on.

I boiled the bone in secret, hastily heating it when Milt was off repairing holes at the Murphy cabin. I could hardly wait for the marrow to soften before I'd scooped the bone out, singeing my fingertips, and sucked at the brown core, desperate for the salvation that lay within. I burned my tongue and tasted nothing. But my stomach gave me peace for a precious few minutes. That was all I needed.

Other days, I made broth of tree bark and leaves. As our bodies' stores sloughed off us, *everything* transformed into a potential meal in my mind. I boiled a leather insole for a full day and a half until it disintegrated, and we ate the soggy pieces of dirty mush, no longer caring for taste, just craving nourishment. Most days, our meals consisted of boiled water and salt.

We were dying.

The wind and sleet were relentless. Our makeshift tarptent was shredded past the point of repair no more than a month into our stay, and we had to move to the Murphy cabin. Being just two, we were lucky: the larger families had to make do in their rapidly deteriorating wagons, for none wanted to take in so many mouths to feed. Indeed, I resented having to share any stock I foraged with the Murphy clan: they were so many, and so hungry! I'd not be able to savor a bite of marrow among this crew.

Milt shook me awake one morning with a gentleness I hadn't felt from him in months. "Lenora," he whispered. "Sweetheart. I have to tell you something."

A week ago, a group of fifteen men had set out in hopes of finding rescue and provisions. I'd tried to use my feminine wiles to convince Milt to go with them, just to get a break from his grating voice and defeatist shrugs, but he'd refused to leave me. I hated him so.

"Have you had word from the party? Are we saved?" I sat up, suddenly wide awake.

"No, dear. No. Nothing like that. It's . . . it's Eleanor."

"What of that mealy mouthed twit? Are they moving in now? There's hardly room for us, shoehorned in this corner. Why can't they impose on the Breens? Their cabin is twice as hardy, and almost as big." I crossed my arms.

"No, Lenora. Stop. Eleanor's gone."

"Gone?" Had that conniving harpy left in the night, off to find food and salvation? A pang of jealousy—or was it hunger?—swept through me.

"She's died, Lenora. Passed away in the night."

"Oh." I thought back to the early days of the journey, when she and I would sit in the sweltering heat, patching britches and darning socks, watching her two boys toddle in the grass. My face fell. She'd had a delightful laugh, one that started in her belly and percolated up through her throat, until it broke free and echoed off the trees and mountains around us. *That* Eleanor was gone.

I did not share the next thought that warmed my heart: *one less to feed.*

I spent the day as I did most others: listless, shivering, unable to muster the energy to do much more than crawl outside to take care of basic bodily functions, though given the lack of nutrients coming *into* our bodies, not much was coming *out*, either. Given the way the white flecks of frozen ice bit at the bare nether-regions, this was the only blessing of our miserable existences. Our cheeks were raw to a man, our lips chapped and cracked, the pots of antelope fat we'd once used to keep mouths moist long since boiled for soup stock. Flaked skin hung from sharp bones, and fewer found the strength with each passing day to even try and chip bark from the stripped trees surrounding us. There were days I prayed not for salvation, but the mercy of death.

I spotted Levinah Murphy creeping out of the cabin at dusk, though with six of her thirteen children huddled around her, moving as one bulky, bumbling unit, *creeping* was nigh on impossible.

"Where are you off to?" I called out. I didn't care if the rest of the cabin heard. The isolation and starvation had made us all suspicious, resentful beasts, and I wanted the rest behind me if she was daring to escape in the night.

"Just over to the other cabin." Her voice was even, but I recognized what the forced calmness of her tone was hiding: hunger.

"What waits there?"

"Please, Lenora," Milt said, stirring next to me. "Be hush. Just let her go."

"I will not." I stood, pulling on my weatherworn boots, seams long since split on the sides. There was but twine and hope holding them together these days. "I'm coming with you."

"You don't want to do that," Milt cautioned.

"I do." I jutted my chin. "Don't you dare presume to know my mind." I strode over to Levinah and her brood. "Let's be off, then."

She looked sad and scared, but clearly she'd had a purpose to her mission. She sighed and herded her children out into the sub-zero wind biting through the darkness. We crossed the slippery path between the cabins without words—there were secrets about, but it would be my eyes, not Levinah's tongue, that would reveal them.

I smelled it before we even climbed the rotting stoop. Even with the frosty wind freezing the nostrils and stealing away scent, it penetrated. Ambrosial tracks teased my senses and caused my mouth to water to the point of drooling in but an instant. It smelled gamy, and full; it promised salty, savory salvation. It was the odor of food. Of meat.

"You cannot go in!" Milt, out of breath, had caught up, and clamped down on my arm hard enough to leave angry purple bruises the next morn.

I wrenched free of his grasp. "You would have me starve!" I accused.

Levinah and the children were already making their way through the door, leaving us to our bitter exchange. *They'll eat it all! We'll die!* I faced Milt and drew back, the full weight of my wrath delivered in a slap across his face. "Leave me be and let me eat!" The words were a scream, pregnant with hate and hunger.

"Stop. We cannot! They've—it's unholy, what they've done. Lenora . . ." The moonlight glistened off of a rapidly freezing tear that clung like a child to his lashes. "They've cooked Eleanor. You see? We *cannot*. We're not monsters."

My mind struggled to grasp at his meaning. *They've cooked Eleanor's what? She had no dog.* Then the cold bathwater of truth washed over me. "They're eating her flesh."

Milt nodded.

The cramping of my withered stomach sprang to life, roaring to a crescendo, ready to do battle with my soul. *We must eat,* it bellowed. *Not like this,* my mind protested. *We are not*—I couldn't even speak the word in my head.

Cannibals. It was a line no God-fearing Christian, no decent soul, could cross.

But the aroma would not stop its meaty assault. It stroked my senses like a tender lover, whispering promises of flavorful salvation, of satiation, of hope. It tickled my tongue, leaving a hint of salt and hickory in its succulent kisses. It reached inside, to my very being, and coaxed out my resolve on a tantalizing leash of promised flesh.

I licked my lips.

No hushed murmurs, no slips of conversation reached us outside the door. *Because they're too busy eating.* My stomach rustled in its lair. *It will be gone soon, and you'll be the next to die. Then they'll eat you, too. Where will your righteous morals have gotten you then?*

I turned to Milt. "We have to eat."

A light left him then, the glimmer I'd first seen on our wedding day, when it danced across his eyes in love and delight as I skipped down the aisle to him. "Lenora." It was a plea.

"Starve if you like. I'm going in." I spun to the door and yanked it wide. I knew he would not follow. I was thankful; Eleanor had wasted away to little more than skin and bones, and I knew the meal of her would not feed many. Let Milt hold on to his morals—more for the rest of us.

And oh, how I ate.

Eating human flesh, once you are able to quash your conscience and let your basic need for survival take over, is not entirely unpleasant. The texture is softly firm, like fresh mushrooms. If prepared correctly—simmered 'til meat falls from bone, not fried to shoe-leather consistency—it is not unlike sweet pork: filling, perhaps a bit difficult to digest, but an eruption of flavor that sets the taste buds afire, especially if one has been subsisting on tree-bark broth for several weeks. It was a feast I hadn't expected to enjoy. But as soon as my fingers plucked the last bits of succulent meat off my plate and I rolled those morsels on my tongue, suckling at the juices, I wanted more.

But for us to gain more bounty and live, someone else had to lose the battle.

When I returned to the Murphy cabin, Milt was already wrapped tight in our thin, frayed blanket. His breathing was clipped, and I knew he was awake, saying nothing. He turned his back to me as I crawled in next to him. No worry: I'd long since lost my desire to be with him. He made an efficient bed-warmer, nothing more.

A man to keep my bed warm at night would be easy enough to replace. I wanted to live.

Some looked guilty the next morning, not wanting to meet gazes as we bustled about camp. But it was that *bustling* that was so important: for so long, an air of listless despair had bled through our every movement. We'd given up on fishing, or keeping the pathways clean; some had even stopped bothering to move more than a few feet away from the cabins before relieving themselves in the snow. Feces and hot yellow holes of piss littered the encampment.

I met every look evenly as I took up a shovel and started clearing away the excrement. Now that my body had known nourishment again, I was unwilling to lay down and die. We needed more food. I tried to remember the sweltering days, so hot the sweat cut a river down our backs. They hadn't been so long ago, had they?

"Lenora." It was Tamsen behind me, and I paused my scooping to return her greeting. "How—how does the day meet you?" She was asking if my conscience had reconciled with my full belly.

"Better than fine, Tamsen." I frowned. "I'm worried about Milt, though. He's weak, and I saw him favoring his left leg this morning. I think his right knee pains him again."

"I'll tend to him, see if I can help," she offered.

"You know Milt. His knee could separate at the bone and he'd deny any injury, even as his leg fell off." I laughed. "Let him be for now."

I studied the drawn figure before me. Her fingertips were blackened with frostbite, and I wondered if they'd have to come off. Franklin Graves had been serving us as a makeshift doctor, though not well: his experience was limited to tending sick oxen. But he could lop off a deadened finger with little ill effect. What had he been doing with those appendages? My eyes narrowed. Was he hoarding his own stew-pot of sustenance?

Probably not fit for consumption, I decided. *We need healthy flesh.*

We need more.

I offered a weak smile to Tamsen, my thoughts fumbling fervently into a plan. "We have other issues at hand."

Tamsen surveyed my shoveling. "Cleaning?"

I shook my head. "No . . . me and Milt. He—" I let my voice drop. "Oh, you mustn't say anything. Promise?" Tamsen nodded, her eyes wide. She did love a good story, and was about as capable of not spreading a tale as a wildfire was of not catching kindling. "We haven't—he has been less husband than brother toward me since setting up camp," I admitted. "And just yesterday, I saw him whispering with Margaret Reed. I dare say—I think he was flirting."

"Oh." Tamsen's voice was resigned. Margaret was quite a beauty, even with her bones pressed against her skin. And her husband James's heavy hand with a whip on his oxen was often whispered of. Our plight had done nothing to ease his short-fused temper.

"I'm sure it was nothing," Tamsen offered.

"I hope you're right." I turned back to the soiled snow before me. "It has me worried, though."

"Of course," Tamsen murmured, and she hurried off, no doubt to churn up the rumor mill.

My cheeks were chafed, my lungs on fire, when I wrested the cabin door shut against the stinging wind. Already my stomach clenched again, demanding sustenance. The meal made of Eleanor hadn't stuck nearly as long as I'd hoped.

From our nest of blankets, Milt's voice called out, a reedy thread. "Lenora? That you?"

Had he really laid there all day? Done *nothing* to try and alleviate our miserable, lice-bitten existence? My eyes narrowed.

"Yes, Milt." I moved closer, wanting to slap him into action. He could've been melting snow for water, or stalking rabbits for dinner, even digging exploratory holes in the snow in search of edible grass or roots. Something.

The door burst open, filling the cabin with angry shouts. James Reed stood, wild-eyed, punctuating his words with a wide-bladed machete he used now to cut through the air as if filleting an antelope. "Where is he? I'll kill that no-good whoreson! Making eyes at *my* Margaret, like a cat stalking a canary! How dare you—dishonor—" His angry words turned to sputters.

Our eyes locked. His were filled with dark intent, a thirst for blood and murder; mine, no doubt, reflected that non-stop craving, the voracious demon in my belly demanding more, more, *more.* I flipped a glance back at Milt, the man I'd once promised before God and our families that I would love, honor, and obey. The man who had spun me around our dusty shanty so long ago and spoke of California dreams, then danced me right into this bone-numbing hellhole. His eyes were sunken, his cheekbones sharp. He looked . . .

. . . delicious.

I stepped aside.

COLOR HIM CRAZY

art James sat among the spectators in the courtroom, listening to the prosecutor's opening statement outlining the case against Bart's little sister. She'd stabbed her boyfriend to death, then barbequed his corpse and eaten it. The prosecutor seemed to think it was an open-and-shut case. In his heart, Bart glumly had to agree. His sister Etta was done for.

The details of the case made Bart sweat. Did crazy run in families? Could *he* be criminally insane, too, his inborn tendencies just waiting for the right time to coil and strike?

He thought of their father, Hank James. Dad had cultivated a wicked sense of humor, the kind of guy that thought it was funny to name his oldest son Jesse, his middle boy Bartles N., and his little girl, Etta. Dumb? Sure. Ensuring that his children would be teased by classmates for life? Without a doubt. But crazy? Bart didn't think giving one's kids ridiculous names quite qualified.

What concerned Bart the most was that Etta was now his second sibling to be arrested for murder. Two years earlier, Jesse had been sent to jail with four life sentences for kidnapping and murdering women. It had been quite the scandal, and Bart had wound up canceling his daily paper when the trial was going on, just to avoid the headlines. It turned out that Jesse liked to cruise the bars in downtown Boston dressed as a cop, pick up young college girls who were too drunk or too unfamiliar with the city to find their way home, and drive them out to deserted areas outside of town. Then he'd strangle them and dump their bodies in the Charles River.

Jesse had been caught due to his own fragile grip on reality, Bart had no doubt. Jesse wound up growing so fond of the Halloween-store cop costume he wore to go hunting for women that he'd taken to wearing it all the time: while mowing the lawn, grocery shopping, even to church. The neighbors complained, and one old woman had called the police asking if it was a crime of some sort, like a stolen valor thing. Some smart deputy had put two and two together—witnesses had seen some of the girls leaving with a costume-store cop, and here was one mowing the lawn; it hadn't taken long for the police to find their man.

During the time that Jesse was on his serial-killer spree, Bart had seen very little of his older brother. Jesse had gotten increasingly harder to talk to over the years, and Bart was often frustrated trying to have a conversation with him. It was difficult for Bart to discuss politics or the economy with a man who insisted that the world was going to hell in a handbasket because "purple." How could Bart argue against that? No, he and Jesse had not been close, and Bart hadn't visited him once in jail since his conviction. Etta mentioned going to see Jesse only one time; when Bart asked how their brother was doing, Etta said, "He's convinced his cellmate is Ronald McDonald, working undercover to expose the prison beef industry. So I'd say he's about the same." They'd discussed it no further.

Now Etta was on trial, accused of a heinous murder. Bart's sister sat at the defendant's table, her short, spiky blue hair clashing with her sedate brown suit. He should've seen the warning signs that Etta was losing her grip on reality. Last year, their mother had been diagnosed with stage four pancreatic cancer, and withered away in a matter of months. On her deathbed, Mom had laid a frail hand on Etta's.

"Sweetheart," their mother rasped, and Etta leaned in to hear her dying wish clearly. "You *really* need to do something with your hair," Mom said, then wheezed and died. Etta took her mother's last words solemnly to heart, and chopped off her silky caramel locks in favor of the prickly blue cropped helmet she wore now.

That was probably not a normal reaction, Bart thought. *The wheel was still spinning, but the gerbil was slowing down even then.*

Etta had started dating Simon Place about two months after Mom had died. Things seemed to be going well, from what Bart could tell. Bart and his wife Mina only saw his sister every other month or so. He was shocked one night to get a call from Gary Hatcher, the James family's longtime attorney, announcing that Etta had been arrested. Bart had kissed Mina goodbye the next morning and made the hour-long drive from his home in Middleborough to the police station in Lowell. Etta had been indignant when he'd finally gotten in to see her in her holding cell.

"He *proposed* to me, Bartles, can you *believe* it?" Etta had stormed. Bart had been confused. Wasn't that a good thing?

Apparently not.

"I've been stuck with a floozy blues singer's name all my life. You think it was easy? Guys singing 'I Just Want to Make Love to You' as soon as they met me? And *then*, when that bimbo re-released 'Something's Got a Hold on Me'? Every day I had people serenading me. Every *day*. Don't get me started, Bartles. You have no idea." She held her hand up, apparently forgetting that her brother had been named after a popular wine cooler, and had taken some ribbing of his own throughout his life.

"So what happened?"

"I told him there was no way I was going to marry a guy with the last name 'Place,'" she said, throwing her hands up in frustration.

"Huh?"

"Jesus, you too? Simon didn't get it, either. Etta Place? Are you kidding me?"

"Still not following," Bart said, frowning.

"Don't you ever read a book? Or even watch old movies? Etta Place was only a huge prostitute that hung out with Butch Cassidy and the Sundance Kid, jackass. I am *not* going to trade my stupid drug-addicted blues singer's name for a big ol' turn-of-the-century hooker's name. No thank you," she said, as if this explained it all.

"So you decided to slit his throat and cook him in Bull's Eye Original instead?" he asked.

"Well, yeah. I was hungry." Etta shrugged.

Brother to both a serial killer and a cannibal. That was Bart's lot in life now. He wished he was home so he could talk to Mina, get her take on the situation. Was she worried at all that he might be secretly nuts? After all, two out of three of the James children had turned out to be murderers. Good lord, what if he and Mina had children? Not that this was even an issue: Bart had always been the sort who preferred pets to people. But what *if?* How would he explain to his children that their aunt and uncle were both killers—not to mention the inherent danger to his imaginary kids. *They* could've been victims. Bart shuddered at the thought. He felt like he'd narrowly escaped a terrible fate.

But *had* he escaped?

Bart didn't know if insanity was genetic. Sure, he'd known growing up that his brother Jesse was weird. His friends' brothers had never painted portraits of JFK on the sides of *their* houses using motor oil and feces. Clearly, Jesse had been an oddball. But Etta? She'd seemed mostly normal.

Mostly normal . . . but not quite, he had to admit. Hadn't Etta once dressed up as Hannibal Lecter for Halloween when she was only ten? Sure, that wasn't so bad, but her insistence that she eat nothing but liver and fava beans for the entire month of October had been a bit extreme. Bart supposed that it had been remarkably strange for a fifth grader. No self-respecting kid that age voluntarily chose to eat liver. And for thirty-one days in a row, no less.

But why had his parents indulged his nutty siblings? Dad, gone now ten years, had always enjoyed a good joke. When Jesse had proudly led his family outside to see his huge JFK oil-and-feces display (and, Bart had to admit, it *had* been impressive in its detail) Dad had roared with laughter. The JFK portrait faced Ed Swann's house, and Ed was something of a ball-buster. Many a night Ed had called the cops on the Jameses to complain that the kids were playing their harpsichords too loudly or that they were setting off fireworks at midnight, in February, in a residential zone. If nothing else, Ed Swann was a bully and a killjoy, and a giant likeness of John Fitzgerald Kennedy made of fecal matter facing Ed's living room window was sweet justice. Dad hadn't been bent out of shape at all that his oldest son had smeared human waste on the side of the house. One good downpour and it had washed away anyway. No harm done.

Bart smiled at the memory of his father. He often wished he could go through life with such an easygoing attitude. His dad had never seemed to worry about mortgages, or that weird noise the car was making, or whether or not the company he worked for was going to survive the recession. Life had thrown curveballs at Hank James from time to time, but he'd just let it all roll right off his back. Bart envied him even now.

His mother, Penelope James, had been another story. She'd been the disciplinarian in the family, and had blown up at Jesse when he'd painted the presidential poo portrait. Jesse had been forced to eat his dinner with a toothpick while keeping two clothespins clamped on his earlobes every night for a week after that incident. Mom had been *tough*. But, theoretically, it should have taught the kids discipline, right? Then why hadn't his brother and sister learned the importance of that one big rule: thou shalt not kill?

Bart couldn't figure it out. Mom had been firm, but fair. Whenever the kids behaved well or got good grades, she made sure they were equally rewarded. Bart still remembered their mother surprising them with handmade bracelets made out of raccoon hair and teeth. Mom had caught, killed, skinned and de-boned the critters herself. *Nothing in the world quite like a mother's love,* he reflected thoughtfully.

Sure, maybe Mom's methods had been a little unorthodox. Probably making Bart eat a floral-scented candle after he stole a Twinkie from the grocery store had been a little extreme. Or forcing Jesse to wear a dress and wig to school after he'd dropped the f-bomb at the dinner table. Hoo, boy, that had taken years for poor Jesse to live down. The school football team had beaten him up every day for a month after that little fiasco. But was forcing your daughter to scrub the toilet with her toothbrush after failing to replace the empty TP roll *really* that uncalled for? Bart was sure other kids had gone through similar punishments—and if they hadn't, they were worse off for it. In any case, it hadn't hurt the James children any, and probably, in the long run, had made them better people.

Bart listened to the prosecutor wrap up his opening arguments. Bart didn't know why Etta was even bothering to fight the charges; the evidence clearly pointed to her, and she'd admitted to Bart himself she'd done it—not that he'd told anybody that. Family was family, and he wasn't about to testify against his little sister. He sighed, folded up the newspaper he'd been reading whenever there was a sidebar, and got up. He was attending the trial to support his sister, but it had already been a long morning. Surely she'd forgive him if he slipped out early to go have lunch with Mina.

Bart left the courthouse and walked down the street to the Walgreens at the corner. He bought a box of Crayolas and some Beggin' Strips, then waited at the bus stop to catch his ride home. He should be there by 12:30, just enough time to have a lazy meal with Mina, discuss his thoughts, and ride back downtown before the afternoon court session started. *Perfect,* he thought.

Mina was lying in bed when he got home. She didn't flit about the house much during the day, and sometimes it seemed to Bart that she spent most of her time just waiting for him to come home. He had some guilt about this, but continued to run his daily errands. After all, nobody wanted to be in another's company twenty-four hours a day, right? *Familiarity breeds contempt,* he reassured himself as he placed the Beggin' Strips and crayons on the kitchen table.

"Mina?" he called gently. "I'm home."

Mina casually sauntered into the kitchen without acknowledging he was even there. She was probably steamed at him for leaving so early this morning without so much as a kiss goodbye. "Don't be mad, babe. I had to run out early; I told you that," he explained as she sat. She watched him with wide brown eyes, but didn't respond.

"Come on. I really need to talk to you about something. I'm worried—well, as you know, both Jesse and now Etta have done some pretty awful things. Are you—do you worry at all, and be honest here, that I might be crazy, too? What if I suddenly went nuts and started threatening people? Killing them, even? Would you still love me? Would you—leave me?" He choked out these last words, burying his head in his hands, both eager for and fearful of what her response might be.

Mina moved over to his side, gently nudging his obscured face.

"Woof," she replied softly, licking his hands. He stared into his wife's face, her chocolate coat shining from the brushing he'd given her the night before. She wagged her tail. "Woof," she repeated again, solemnly.

Well, that was a relief.

Bart kissed Mina sloppily on the cheek and began serving lunch. He placed four Beggin' Strips on a plate for Mina, then selected blue violet, burnt sienna, tan, and screamin' green for his own plate. They munched on their respective lunches in silence.

"At least we have each other," he sighed, finally. Mina looked at him and panted, letting her tongue loll out. "Don't do that," he chastised her gently. "You look ridiculous."

POPULAR

The young girl's left hand, the one holding the pregnancy test, trembles. *Tonight*, Amy Nesmith decides. *Tonight, after school, before dinner, is when I'll do it. Good a time as any to kill myself.*

She blinks at her reflection in the mirror. How could she have been so stupid? To think Jeff Kendall might have actually *liked* her? Amy studies her wide brown eyes, her poker-straight dishwater hair. Had she really felt pretty when Jeff asked her out? *I don't know if you're into hockey*, he'd said. *Yes—yes, I am*, she'd said, her smile so wide she'd worried the corners of her mouth would split. She's had a crush on Jeff since freshman year. The moment had been surreal, her grinning like an idiot in her low-cut, maybe-a-little-too-tight purple sweater she'd found at Savers that her mother hadn't wanted her to buy, but from this moment on Amy would deem it forever her lucky purple sweater . . .

I have tickets to see the Bruins Friday night, Jeff had said. She'd started nodding before he even got out *Do you want to go with me?*

I love the Bruins! Ray Bourque—

Ray Bourque retired, like, before we were born.

I know, my point is, I just love Bruins hockey. Yes. Thank you. I'd love to go.

And after—and after . . .

Of course she'd had sex with him after. She'd spent almost three years surreptitiously searching for him between classes in the hallway, only to quickly glance away if he happened to look in her direction. Amy's one friend, Lauren Francis, had once asked if they could have a day—just one *afternoon*, really, a couple hours at most—in which they could talk about anything else *but* Jeff Kendall. And Amy hadn't been able to do it. So this date, the hockey game and then after, when he'd parked his car down at the end of the dirt road behind the dump . . . it was everything she'd hoped for since she'd first laid eyes on Jeff in gym class their freshman year.

There was no way Amy *wouldn't*—she'd wanted him to *like* her—of course she'd put out.

Why would you think he'd ever like you? She frowns at her pointy chin, her hooked nose. Her two front teeth overlap so badly it is impossible to eat anything without getting some particle of her meal stuck there. *Stupid.* The angry, venom-filled voice in her head is enough to drive the tears back. *You're so stupid; you deserve this.*

That stupid purple V-neck. *Lucky, my foot. He asked you out because that sweater made you look like a—a slut, and he knew he'd*—her eyes fill with tears. *Stupid!*

"What's taking so long?" Her mother's muffled voice calls

through the closed door of the bathroom.

She glances once more at her sharp features, pocketing the e.p.t. "Just thinking how much I look like a witch," Amy says.

"Don't be ridiculous. There's no such thing as witches."

But Amy knows that there *are* such things as witches. She knows this, because she passes them in the hallway every day.

Poppy Anderson, Cookie Matthews, and Evie Saint. Lauren calls them the Witches of Eastbrook. In private, Amy thinks of them as Poopie, Kooky, and Evil. She knows it's petty and childish. But this is a hellfire trio of the meanest girls to ever trod God's green earth. Amy and Lauren can't walk by them without being stung by their barbs.

"Nice outfit, Nesmith. I see Kmart had a clearance sale again."

"Hold up a minute, Lauren. I want to play connect the dots with the zits on your face." Poopie even approached Lauren that time, Sharpie uncapped and poised, ready to draw on the girl's cheeks.

The taunts don't stop. The tripping, the accidentally-on-purpose elbows to the ribs, the jeering, never ends. Amy's hatred of them lies coiled in a reptilian ball in her stomach, ready to lash out futilely at the sight of the girls, fangs snapping at air. She can't understand why everyone at Eastbrook High doesn't hate the trio. But there's always a small crowd by the witches' lockers, hangers-on and lackeys hoping that the glow of the witches' popularity will somehow shine on them.

Amy and Lauren are not popular. Not by a long shot. It is this reason alone that Amy knows she should've known better than to trust Jeff Kendall. *Guys like him do not fall in love with girls like you. Ugly girls. Slouchy, average girls who yes, do buy new outfits only when there's a clearance at Kmart.*

No matter. Tonight, all of her problems will go away. She'll walk to Cotton Hollow after school. There's a waterfall there, a particularly rough and shallow one, and last summer, Corky Beauchemin broke his neck diving off the top. He's not the first kid who died trying to perform such a feat. If Amy has her way, he will not be the last.

Now that she has a plan in place, she feels liberated. The weight of the world is off her shoulders. She opens the bathroom door and breezes past her mother.

"Hurry up or you'll miss the bus," Mom says.

Amy kisses her cheek. "Thanks, Mom. Goodbye."

Amy meets Lauren in front of the school where the buses let the students off for the day. They always walk in together: a united duo against the witches.

"You seem chipper today," Lauren says. Lauren is chubby and dark and has an unfortunate mole on her chin, which she usually (but not always) remembers to pluck the one wiry hair from when it sprouts.

"I am." Amy smiles. "I couldn't really tell you why." *Because you might find it alarming, and I won't let you talk me out of it,* she silently adds. They walk up the steps together, Lauren chatting away about last night's episode of *American Horror Story,* Amy nodding but not hearing the words. *None of this matters. Not us, not me. Lauren'll be sad when I'm gone, sure, but she'll be fine. Probably get some sympathy from my death, and she'll be less of a target. She'll be better for it when I'm dead.*

Poopie, Kooky, and Evil are in their designated spot, huddled in a circle by their lockers. *All they're missing is a cauldron,* Amy thinks. But wait—they do have one of sorts, a pink plastic bucket that Evil holds steady as Kooky stirs the contents with a wooden spoon. Evil glances up at Amy and Lauren as they try to slip by, and there's a quick jerk of the hands. Amy barely has time to blink before Lauren catches a bucket of grape Kool-Aid square in the chest. Amy is splattered—her pretty pale yellow shirt is now ruined—but Lauren is drenched. The soaked girl makes sharp hiccupping noises deep in her throat as if trying to swallow the sobs before they break surface. Amy wipes the grape droplets from her eyes with the corner of her sleeve, and looks at Evil. And laughs.

"Is that the best you can do? Really?"

"Sorry," Evil says, but there is no hint of remorse in the word. "It slipped."

"Doesn't matter. None of this matters. *You* don't matter." Amy jabs a finger close to Evil's grin, and the moon-faced girl snaps her teeth, pretending to try and take a bite. Amy doesn't care. There are bigger problems that can happen besides a Kool-Aid bath. Like being pregnant at seventeen by a guy who hasn't called you since the night you put out after the Bruins-Rangers match.

Evil flips Amy off, but Kooky takes a step closer and studies Amy's face. A smile tugs at one corner of her perfectly lipsticked mouth. "Go on," Kooky murmurs.

"Piss off," Amy says shakily. She links her arm through Lauren's. Lauren is crying now, which Amy hates—*don't give them that power*—and the two of them head into the girls' lavatory to wipe off as best they can. Lauren will smell like sickly grape sugar all afternoon.

Amy avoids the witches for the rest of the day. It's easy enough to do—she's in all the average classes, and the witches are overachievers, on the college track. High math. AP English. Amy doesn't even have to see them at lunch. She suspects all of the smart kids have their own scheduled feeding time, when they refuel with flaxseed and omega-3 fish oils and all that other brain food. Amy lifts up her pizza square and takes a bite. *My last cafeteria pizza. I won't miss this, either.*

She can think of nothing she *will* miss in her life. Her father left years ago, no forwarding address, no token gifts at Christmas, no child support. And it seems like Amy and her mother fight all the time these days—her mom doesn't get that cheap Kmart clothes and Cutting Crew haircuts are neon "loser" signs to the rich kids that grace the halls of Eastbrook High. "Nobody ever gave me anything," her mother likes to say. "If you want nicer clothes, go out and get a job."

But Amy can't get a job, because she doesn't have a car to get there. She babysits once in a while, but not enough to save any money, and besides, she hates kids. *Reason number one million and one to get this over with. I can't imagine having to take care of a screaming brat every day.*

She takes another bite, tasting warm, slightly burnt cheese, dough, and slick, seasoned grease. She eyes the glistening square. *Maybe I will miss the school pizza,* she decides.

But just this. Only this.

Amy deliberately doesn't catch the bus home after school.

Cotton Hollow is maybe a three mile walk. She sets out, head down, shoulders slumped, hands in pockets, as a light rain starts to fall. The path to the Hollow is easy to miss—just a thin dirt trail off the main road, narrower than a bike lane. Amy keeps her eyes trained on the side of the road, and her heart jumps when she sees the thin strip of trodden earth lying in wait amid the yellowing grass. She takes a quick look around before ducking down the path, disappearing between the pines.

The forest works well enough as an umbrella, and she slips her hood from her head. The woods are silent, as is she. Her heart drums in her ears as she walks. *Thum-thud, thum-thud.* Is there a second heartbeat there? She shakes her head—she refuses to think of such things. What's done is done, and her mind is made up. She pulls out a stick of Juicy Fruit, and in a moment, all she hears is her own chewing. Her eyes stay focused on the needle-laden path before her as she makes her way to the wide stream.

The roar of the water makes her look up as she nears. There it is: a cascading waterfall of ink hiding a deadly secret beneath what appears to be a deep pool at the base, where less than a foot of water masks a run of granite stone. The very spot where Corky broke his neck less than a year earlier; the spot where she intends to take her own life in a swan dive now. Someone— likely the town—has put up a new sign, white with CAUTION! NO SWIMMING! in red.

And across the bank, a figure, ethereal in black, arms crossed: Kooky Matthews. "Well, screw me," Amy mutters, pulling out her gum and sticking it to the back of the caution sign.

Kooky is upon her in a flash, as if she's crossed the falls like the savior walking on water. Amy's *mad* now. How dare this sick troll interrupt her plans? Did Kooky follow her? How dare she? Amy wants to scratch this shrew's perfectly proportioned face, claw her eyes out, throttle her for daring to ruin her afternoon. This was *her* special moment. Kooky is not supposed to be a part of it.

"You're pregnant," Kooky says.

"Am not," Amy lies. "Go away. You're the last person I want to see right now."

"I can help you," Kooky continues, as if Amy hasn't spoken. "Take care of that for you."

Amy has a vision of a dimly lit room and a coat hanger. "No, thank you. Goodbye now." She juts out her chin and points down the path she's just traipsed to get here. "Go."

Kooky doesn't move. She places two cold hands on Amy's cheeks, and stares so intensely into her eyes that Amy fears Kooky will kiss her. "You don't want this baby," Kooky says.

"No." The truth escapes as a sob before Amy can bite it back.

"You'd rather die first."

"Yes," Amy whispers.

In one swift motion, Kooky reaches down and sinks her cold fingers into the flesh of Amy's stomach. Kooky wrenches her hand, as if turning a handle, and a sharp stab from a phantom scalpel hooks through Amy's abdomen. Amy doubles over in pain—her insides are knotted and twisted, searing agony shooting hot tendrils through her intestines, down to her crotch. The pain is too much—Amy falls to her knees, shaking.

Kooky mirrors her fall, kneeling down with her, hand still pinching belly. She takes a long, deep breath, as if inhaling Amy's pain, her very soul.

The cramping starts. Amy can't hide the tears now. She

thinks she is dying. She can feel dampness in her panties.

Kooky gasps, then releases her hold. She runs a chilled, bony palm down Amy's back. "There. Better now, right?"

At her words, the cramps ease slightly. Amy snakes a hand down the front of her pants, then pulls it back out. Bright red blood kisses her fingertips.

"How . . ." she shakes her head. She doesn't care how. The ground is hard beneath her, and she's certain she's now no more pregnant than the brittle chunk of wood, etched with blackened termite holes, that lies before her in the dirt. "Why would you help me?"

"Ah, but *you've* helped *me*," Kooky says. She closes her eyes for a moment, inhaling sharply again, her tongue flicking dampness across her lip, resembling a sated lioness after a feast. She opens her eyes and narrows her lids, as if remembering that this is loathsome Amy Nesmith in front of her, not her friend—never her friend. Her mouth pulls back in a wicked smile. "Now let me help *you*."

"Can you—*are* you a witch? Can you make me pret—"

"Popular." The word drips from Kooky's mouth like hot solder, and she licks her thumb, stamping her spit on Amy's forehead.

Amy shrugs. She'll take it.

The walk home is a haze. Once she pops out of the Cotton Hollow path and back onto the main road, she calls her mom to come pick her up. She apologizes for not telling her she was going to the Hollow after school. She swears she thought she said something that morning. Her mother wants to argue about it, but Amy has no fight left in her. She simply nods when her mother tells her she'll have to sweep and mop the kitchen floor as punishment. She'll hum the song from *Cinderella* when she's pushing the broom, she decides. *Cinderelly, Cinderelly, who's not preggers, Cinder-elly*, she thinks, stifling a gleeful giggle.

When she gets home, Amy runs into the bathroom, fishing out a tampon from the box and saying a silent prayer of thanks. *I'll never complain about PMS again, Lord. I promise.*

She almost promises to never say anything bad about the Witches of Eastbrook again, but stops herself. Yes, Kooky has just done her a huge favor. But things can't just change overnight.

Amy stares at the e-mail counter on her phone the next morning: 2,115 new messages.

Her account must've been hacked. She clicks on the little blue icon with the white envelope, unsure who to contact about this. Google? Verizon?

Friend requests and follows. From Instagram, TikTok, Snapchat. E-mail notifications of new Twitter followers. She thumbs up her Twitter feed. She now has over a thousand followers.

Yesterday, she had twenty-six, most of them bots.

What's going on?

She pads down to the bathroom and scoops cold water over her face. She looks in the mirror. Same hook nose, same pointy chin. She has a serious case of bedhead this morning. Nothing has changed.

Hackers. Has to be. She dresses quickly and shouts a goodbye to her mother as she flies out the door.

On the bus, she shrugs down into a seat and fishes in her backpack for her earbuds, which help drown out the loneliness of not being spoken to morning after morning. A shadow falls across the seat, and she looks up to see Kyle Goggins looming over her. Normally, he'd be sneering or mouthing a taunt, but today, he's smiling, and not meanly.

Surely he's mistaken her for someone else.

"Scooch over?"

She glances around at the near-empty bus—she's the second one on, Kyle the third, and there are plenty of empty seats. "Huh?"

"Oh, you're saving it for someone. Of course—sorry."

"No," she says too quickly, and still rushing: "You can sit here." She slides over.

"Thanks." He's grinning wider now. He asks if she's read *The Long Earth* yet for English. Kyle sits two seats over from her in Mr. Sellman's class. She shakes her head.

"Me neither. It's like they're trying to kill any desire we might have to pick up a book by forcing us to read the most boring crap ever written. What do you like to read?"

Amy blinks at him. Nobody has ever asked before. Nobody has ever . . . cared.

Kyle likes sci-fi. "I'm really into Jim Butcher right now. Ever heard of him?" Amy says in a shaky voice (*what is going on here?*) that she mostly sticks to graphic novels, he asks her what's her favorite and when she says *Ghost World*, he immediately brings it up on his phone and one-click buys it so they can talk about it tomorrow.

More kids get on the bus. The Lee twins, Andre and

Murray, slide into the seat behind her and Kyle. Andre gives her a light tap on the shoulder and tells her she looks cute today. Amy shakes off the compliment—it's obviously a joke, and not a very nice one, but . . . Heather Russo and Kelly Maguire take the seat across the aisle. Heather immediately asks Amy if she's going to the school football game that weekend. Does she need a ride? Does she want to go with her and Kelly?

Amy looks around. Normally, at the end of the route, most kids on the bus are sitting alone, faces pointing at phones. Today, they're all clustered in one section. Around her.

The crowd does not disperse once the driver lets them off at school. She sees Lauren's eyes go wide at the bodies chatting, laughing, moving *en masse* around Amy.

"Get in here," Amy calls out. Lauren just shakes her head, blinking at the crowd passing by, Amy still at the center.

The horde clogs the hallway in a circle around Amy's locker. "Have you heard the new Drake song? Here, I'll text you the link," Gretchen Paulson says.

"Snapchat selfie!" Suzanne Jackson hooks her chin over Amy's shoulder, and her iPhone flashes. "I just found the puppy dog filter—it's sooo cute. You'll love it. I'll tag you in it," she says as Amy blinks away the spots in her vision.

"Walk with me to homeroom," Felix Neville insists. He throws an arm over Amy's shoulder, like they've been besties for years. Up until this moment, he has never spoken one word to her, and they've been sitting next to each other in homeroom for three years now.

Her heart catches as she recognizes the Prussian blue eyes and white-blond hair parting the crowd. "Morning, doll." Jeff Kendall plucks Felix's arm off Amy's shoulder and leans in, kissing her. "I know you two are buds, but don't get *too* friendly with my girl," he adds, glaring at Felix, who laughs nervously. Jeff flashes his dimples at Amy. "Text me later?"

This is the same guy who *used* her—somehow caught wind of gigantic, enormous, and okay, probably totally obvious crush on him, let's face it, she did doodle *I luv Jeff K* on the knee of her ripped jeans a few times, and maybe she talked about him nonstop, it's not like she and Lauren didn't talk in the hallways like everyone else in the world, so sue them, and anyone could've heard—but this guy, he . . . well, he ghosted her. Got what he wanted and never called her again, never answered her texts. He's a total player. Amy should be furious. Should tell him to piss off, that just that morning a guy had downloaded a *chick* book based on her recommendation alone. Jeff hadn't asked her once what she was into at all on their date, had only asked how big she thought—had left her *pregnant*, for goodness sake—but . . .

"Uh, okay," Amy stutters.

Crushes since freshman year gym class don't die overnight.

Kooky's hiss rings in her ears. *Popular.*

And where are the Witches of Eastbrook this morning? Amy cranes her neck to try and get a glimpse of them before Felix can steer her away. She thinks she sees Poopie out of the corner of her eye. Snickering.

In homeroom, they're supposed to fill out an updated emergency contact form, but Felix won't shut up long enough to let Amy read it. He's not the only one. Olivia Neidel, to her left, slips her a note asking her if she *likes* Felix. For Christ's sake! He's looked *through* her for three years, and now he won't stop talking—she's ready to kill him, not date him! She shakes her head at Olivia and then Felix is tugging on her sleeve to tell her more about the fascinating lacrosse practice he had yesterday.

Amy scribbles her mother's cell phone number on the form. Randy Neelson jumps up, scooping up her form and turning it in for her along with his own.

Mercifully, the bell rings.

On the way to her first class, the crowd forms again, bombarding Amy with questions. "What do you think about . . ."

"Would you ever go out with . . ."

"I love your shirt. Where did you get it?" Amy glances up. That one comes from Evil Saint as she walks by, and Amy doesn't think she cares one iota about Amy's blue-light special blouse.

Amy makes it to math class and takes her seat. She sighs in relief—the crowd can't follow her in here, right? They're not *all* in algebra.

Maribeth Miller sits down next to her.

In the seat that's been vacant all semester.

Lowell Gutierrez, whose wiry neck hairs Amy has stared at since fall, swivels around to talk to her.

"What're you doing sixth period? You have that free, right? Want to run over to Mickey D's with me and Adnan?"

"You're kidding, right?" Amy blurts. "Do you even know my name?"

"You're funny," Lowell says with a wink. "Like we haven't been BFFs all semester."

Bizarro world. Is this what it's like? To have people want to spend time with you, care about your opinion? The butterflies in her stomach—not baby kicks, thank God—are flapping in exhilaration. And terror. She hasn't talked to this many people in one day . . . ever. What if she says something stupid, and everyone realizes she's still the same old loser?

"So you're coming, right?" Lowell asks. Amy blinks, then nods. What's it like to leave campus and grab McNuggets with friends in the middle of the day? She doesn't know. But it sounds like fun (*what if McNuggets are for babies and everyone else gets a Big Mac?* the butterflies thrum). She swallows, and decides she wants to experience it, before she wakes up and her newfound popularity is gone, lost with the first bite of a fried chicken turd.

People surround her all day. In the cafeteria, Tyler Zweifel pulls three tables together so everyone can sit with Amy at lunch. The goths, the jocks, the brains and the drama geeks . . . *everyone* wants her time. Her attention. She can't even eat her mashed potatoes, because every time she lifts her fork to her mouth, someone asks her another question. Why are they so fascinated? These people who have ignored her for so long? The attention is nice. More than that—it's addictive. But she's starving by the end of the day. Even her sixth period Mickey D run leaves the butterflies unfed, Adnan and Lowell snatching up her McNuggets and dipping them into her mustard sauce while they ask her about her plans for the weekend, if she's seen the new Dwayne Johnson movie yet, if she wants to . . .

She accepts a ride home from Olivia Neidel. Except Ollie wants to stop at the mall first. Then the Lee twins meet up with them, and they all go to Kidzone to play Whack-a-Mole for cheap plastic prizes even though she's sure they'll think it's stupid when she suggests it. Then Jeff shows up and wants to drive around town together but he doesn't even try to get in her pants this time. Okay, she does let him go up her shirt, but he doesn't push it any further, and she wonders if she's done something wrong, but he seems happy, asking her about her day and if she wants to come over and Netflix and chill tomorrow after school. He drops her off at home, close to ten.

Her mother is furious that she was out so late without even a phone call. Amy won't be Netflixing or anything tomorrow, because she's grounded, young lady.

There's a surprising twinge of relief that comes with the words *you're grounded*. Amy's had no time today to do *anything*. She missed the algebra test review because Lowell and Maribeth were whispering at her the whole time. She flubbed a question in English class because Kyle was making faces at her, giving her the giggles. She hasn't done one page of homework, and can't now; it's past her bedtime. She's starving—she was too busy answering questions and giving her opinion and looking at pictures and having people laugh at her jokes for the first time in her life to have more than a mouthful or two of anything.

She hasn't talked to or even texted Lauren all day.

Amy's exhausted. But now she's home—she can take a minute to *breathe*. She inhales sharply, thinking of Kooky the day before in the woods, the sound of her pulling in air like she was gorging on the very life essence of it.

Maybe she was.

Well, Amy can text Lauren now, fill her in on this crazy day and maybe even warn her, because now Amy's convinced: the Witches are real. She grabs a box of cheese crackers and checks her phone, the first time since early this morning that she's actually had a chance to look at it.

412 unread posts in Facebook Messenger.

1,901 private messages in her Twitter notifications.

3,398 new Instagram messages.

6,877 new texts.

12,022 new e-mails.

She'd turned her phone on silent when the texts had started rolling in when she was on the bus with Kyle. They're still popping up, banner notifications of messages from numbers she doesn't recognize, all with a tone of familiarity as if she's been friends with these people for years. Amy feels the energy draining from her with each new text and e-mail. She can't do this. Can't *pay attention* to all of these people demanding her time. If Lauren even tried calling or messaging, Amy can't tell—it's too far buried in all the other PMs. She can't even open an app to play a round of Pet Rescue without the messages buzzing by, bumping the game into pause mode as each one comes in. She tries to open the settings on her phone to turn the banner notifications off, but they keep coming, an endless stream thwarting her navigation.

A new message fills the screen, momentarily silencing the rest: *How does it feel? To be popular?*

Kooky.

I want my life back, Amy types furiously. *Now.*

You wanted to take your life yesterday. Fickle, aren't we?

I didn't know what you were doing. You said you were giving me something.

I did. I gave you the ability to recognize that your life wasn't so bad.

Amy sighs. She's in no mood for some stupid "every life has meaning" lesson from this crazy witch. *You've made your point. Can things please go back to the way they were now? I'll take the Kool-Aid bath.*

There's a moment of blessed, blissful silence. Then the next message comes through:

I don't think you've fully grasped the situation. This wasn't some teachable It's a Wonderful Life *moment. You thought being pregnant was bad. You should've shut up and been happy with what you had. Now it's too late.*

And tomorrow? Your popularity will increase threefold. Consider it a gift from the Witches of Eastbrook.

Amy Nesmith blinks at her reflection in the mirror. She's shut off her phone, because her new friends won't leave her alone. It hasn't helped. First Ollie, then Kyle, then Jeff and Adnan and Suzanne and Lowell and the Murray twins stopped by the house this morning, knocking on the front door just to check in, to see if she needs a ride, or to hang out before school.

Her mother let them in. She didn't know any better. The din in the living room is deafening, and getting louder with each new knock at the door.

Tonight, Amy decides. *Tonight, after school, before dinner, is when I'll do it. Good a time as any to kill myself.*

FREE TO GOOD HOME

You thought you were cooler than iced cappuccino when you got that high-paying job as a software engineer, cramming your bed and your couch and your Xbox into a U-Haul and hauling your whole life up to Bar Harbor. Had a full three weeks of snapping pictures of your fabulous new world, posing with a chocolate mojito at the hottest downtown night club, smiling wide at the snow-covered shore, posting it all on Insta and Twitter with hashtags like #uwishuwereme and #itsamainething. Then—

—well, then. The pandemic of course.

Your happy little Insta world came crashing down as one week, two, a month, two months slipped by, and suddenly working from home has become your new normal and you can't remember the last time you saw another person's face. A *whole* face, not the teenage cashier's two frightened eyes too skittish to meet yours above a hand-sewn mask at Hannaford's. And you don't want to meet the kid's eyes, either, because he knows how much beer you've been buying, you're in here every other day loading up on enough to host a frat party for a week.

It's during one of those beer-fueled long nights (and they seem longer here than where you're from, whose bright idea was it to move north anyway) that you find her online: your savior. A black-and-white knight in shining armor, if saviors and knights come advertised on Facebook Marketplace as *FREE TO GOOD HOME: 1YO SHEPHERD-TERRIER MIX, SPAYED*, and you suspect they do.

You wrap up in your puffy winter jacket and your knit hat that you'd never be caught dead in when posting pics online, and of course your mask and gloves, can't go anywhere without those these days or you'd be shot dead in the street, and you drive to Blue Hill to meet this black and white mottled darling, and within two hours you are serenading this *1YO SHEPHERD-TERRIER MIX, SPAYED* as she sits in her crate in the back seat. Her paws are crossed delicately in front of her and she seems to have no objections to your off-key rendition of Blind Melon's "No Rain" and already you love her.

You name her Molly Jones, mostly because "Ob-La-Di, Ob-La-Da" is your favorite Beatles song, plus giving her a formal first and last name makes you giggle. You used to have a more finely tuned sense of humor, you suspect, but it has been a long pandemic so far and besides, Molly Jones thinks you're hilarious. You order special grain-free dog food from Petco's delivery service, then read an article that night about how grain-free is terrible for dogs and call to return it the next day. The girl on the phone explains how in less than a day three of her coworkers have quit including her manager, and delivery is no longer an option. After she apologizes for curbside pickup only now, and you don't verbally abuse her, she starts reading labels aloud in a sing-song voice to you until she hits upon one that is full of grain, designed specifically for dogs under six years of age, promotes good teeth and glossy coats and is easy to digest and sure, costs twice as much as the other stuff, probably because of all the added grain, but nothing's too good for Molly Jones.

She is now, utterly, your world.

The Petco girl on the phone has been so helpful, you figure you can ask her to throw in some treats and some chewies and maybe pick out a few squeaky toys, something the Petco girl thinks would be suitable for a *1YO SHEPHERD-TERRIER MIX, SPAYED*. Heck, she's the expert, she works there, right? You drive back for your curbside return and pickup, and Petco girl is actually Petco lady, has to be well into her fifties with slumped shoulders and split ends, but you tip her twenty bucks anyway because she is so nice. Molly Jones barks at her from the passenger seat as the woman loads your purchases into the way back. Petco lady gives a laugh and a wave, taps the back of your Rogue after she closes the door to send you on your way, and you're certain she's smiling under that mask. She was so chatty on the phone, so eager to shop for you. You bet she's lonely during this whole global plague, and debate calling her later to advise her to get a dog. Maybe after you've had a couple beers.

Molly Jones is whining from her seat, pawing at the upholstery like she means to jump over two rows of seats to get at the bag in back. You start singing "No Rain" again to try and distract her even though it's not on the radio this time. She whines louder and you sing louder and then the most amazing thing happens: Molly Jones looks at you, cocks her head to the side for a moment, then puts her nose in the air, arches her back, and howls. You're so surprised you stop mid-chorus.

The dog stops.

You start again, fumbling for the words, but Molly Jones doesn't care, her howls start right up as soon as you belt out "So stay some-*thing* something to-daaaayy" which is wrong and the lead singer is spinning in his grave right now but who cares, Molly Jones is singing with you and your dog is a genius!

Back at the house, you put the bag down on the kitchen table and unclick Molly Jones's leash. She immediately puts her paws up on the rim, practically knocking the round Ikea two-seat café tabletop over. "Okay, okay, girl. Calm down. We'll see what Petco picked out for you in a minute. Let me take off my boots." It feels good to have someone to talk to again besides your boss, who only checks in once a week to get a status report on the jobs you're working, and only half-listens when he does. Molly Jones is an attentive audience, and *she* thinks you're fascinating.

You pull out a bag of Wag Jerky and Molly Jones goes nuts, crying her high-pitched whine and spinning in circles. You suspect she's seen these before, maybe not this exact brand but she clearly knows what treats are. After all, she is a 1YO *SHEPHERD-TERRIER MIX, SPAYED,* not a brand-new puppy, and the nice old man who was moving to Pennsylvania to stay with his son during this pandemic did seem awfully sad to let his good girl go. You feel a pang of jealousy that someone else had any time with Molly Jones before you, sad that you spent a whole year of her existence without her, and a little voice in the back of your mind says *do you hear yourself? You really need to be around people again* but you ignore it because you're too busy pulling open the bag to give Molly Jones a snack.

You hold it up and say "Sit!" and she does because Molly Jones is the smartest dog in the world and that nice old man clearly put some effort into training your little girl for you.

As Molly Jones chomps away at her treat, you reach back in the bag and feel something fuzzy and soft. "What's this? Who's a pretty baby who wants a new toy?" You're talking baby talk but what the hell, who cares at this point? Who's going to hear you? "What is it, Molly Jones? What's your new toy?" You pull out a plush brown rabbit. The tag says "Four squeakers for extra fun!" and yes, Molly Jones deserves four squeakers, she *sang along with you in the car.* The dog starts her spinning-whining routine again and you laugh, because she's so darn cute when she does that, and you pull off the tag and hand it to her. "It's a bunny! We'll call it Bunny." You've reached the pinnacle of your creative naming abilities when you named Molly Jones, and besides, the dog doesn't care. She grabs Bunny out of your hand and growls as she shakes it back and forth in her jaws.

"Good girl," you say, and while Molly Jones is distracted, you duck into the pantry off the kitchen and pull out the rest of the bag's contents. There's a braided rope and a fat green frog promising even more squeaks, this time with crinkly webbed feet. You put Ropey and Froggy up on the top shelf of the pantry closet for later, and hustle back to the living room to play with your new dog.

"Where is Bunny's face?"

Molly Jones cocks her head, looking at you wide-eyed, ears perked.

An exploded cloud of white stuffing litters the couch and floor. What was once Bunny is now a shell of a rabbit, a half-hollowed skin of brown fur and ears, and its embroidered bunny cheeks and delicate pink nose are gone. Just gone.

"You ate Bunny's face?"

Molly Jones wags her tail.

You sigh, trudge back to the pantry to retrieve Ropey, then pull out the vacuum to clean up the massacre.

Your Insta posts are now all filled with images of Molly Jones. She is sleeping in one, chewing Froggy's face off in another. Here is the dog panting after a jog on the beach, snow now melted. Surely the pictures bring your followers as much joy as they bring you. You change your profile photo to one of Molly Jones in which she looks kind of like she's smiling.

You order at least four more plush toys before you realize it's futile; Molly Jones will simply eat their faces and leave their stuffing entrails all over the house. You're tired of vacuuming every other day, so you switch to strictly tug toys and rubber balls. It's probably better for her teeth anyway, not to mention her bowels. Sometimes she poops fuzz. The dog doesn't bark or jump quite as high for these non-stuffed wares, so you decide she can rip off a face or two on very special occasions.

Your boss still checks in regularly and you're still keeping up with your work, though it does seem like expectations are lower now. On a Zoom meeting with your team, you notice Amber's roots are coming in, and she isn't wearing makeup. Gregory might not even be wearing pants, though you can't swear to that. Molly Jones pops her head up during your meeting and your coworkers ooh and aah and laugh, confirming for you that she is, in fact, the cutest, smartest, most loveable dog in the world, just as you've suspected from the start. You try to get her to sing on-camera but your boss says another time, you all have to get back to work. After you disconnect (and double-check three times to make sure you really *are* disconnected) you scratch behind Molly Jones's ears for a full three minutes. "Today's status report is that Molly Jones is the cutest, smartest dog in the world again today, team," you say, and you get a wet slobbery kiss on the cheek from a velvety doggie tongue in return. "Now leave us alone with your pesky work nonsense!"

Spring is summer is fall and for each holiday, you call up Petco and your friend there picks out a special something just for Molly Jones. (Now that you have someone else to take care of, you're drinking less, and tip Petco lady more.) Your delightful little girl rips the face off Chicky for Easter, and Kitty on Memorial Day. There is no animal suitable for Independence Day, Petco explains sheepishly, but no worries— Molly Jones happily eats the face off the sloth wearing a red, white, and blue tie that Fourth of July.

She growls in delight when she eats Turkey's head that November, and you'd scold her for the absolute desecration of your Rudolph decoration at the holidays, but even your estranged father snorts his approval and says "I've always hated that reindeer" on the family Christmas Zoom call.

Molly Jones is a very good girl. You post a video of her howling along to your rendition of "Come Again" by Damn Yankees (Molly Jones likes them better than Blind Melon, you've found) and get 126 likes, and @welovedogs and @shepherdspirit start following you on TikTok.

You read the headlines online in January and your heart sinks. Vaccines mean *back to the office*, which means no more days working at home with Molly Jones snuggled on your lap.

As the rollouts start you're happy you're young and won't be able to get your shots until late spring. But then the availability estimates are sooner and sooner and the clouds seem darker and gloomier on your daily walks with the dog.

Molly Jones can sense something coming, that's for sure. You give her more treats and toys and even though she's happy to rip them apart, now she slinks off to her crate when she's done, a bit of fuzz still stuck to her nose as she looks at you with sorrowful eyes. How can you leave her?

Your boss calls to give you the rundown on what the company expects. They'll start the return slowly, maybe two days a week in the office and they're spacing out seating so everyone will feel safe. "I can't," you say. "I'm not ready."

Your boss says he understands, but it's not his choice, it's the company directive, and they're mostly concerned that over a year working from home has taken its toll on employees' mental health. Would you like information about the employee counseling program?

You would not. You start to cry, big, hitching, full-body sobs that your boss gets to hear up close in the receiver. "Jesus, Smith. Are you sure you're okay?"

You just want to stay home with your dog.

"Well, it's not happening tomorrow. You have a little time. You can get the dog into a new routine."

"Her name," you say indignantly, "is Molly Jones."

"I'm sorry, Smith. You're out of time," your boss says, his third call that week. "Mandatory two days in starts next week."

"I can't," you say. You can hear the tears in your own voice and you hate yourself for it, but you look at Molly Jones, who is looking at you with those big brown eyes begging you to say it isn't so, and you can't help yourself. "I can't leave her!"

"Okay. Okay," your boss says. "I talked to Human Resources and worked it out so that you can bring her in with you the first week. Will that help? If she's with you that first week? Ease you into the transition?"

He's an okay guy, your boss. "Yes," you whisper. "That would help. Thank you."

"She stays on the leash, though."

Molly Jones hates her leash. But once your boss sees how cute and perfect she is, he won't care anymore about a stupid leash, you're sure. "Of course," you say.

You arrive back at the office the following Tuesday with Molly Jones tugging on her leash. You packed a bag for her with bowls for water, food, several treats, Ropey 2 (Ropey 1 frayed away months ago, may he rest in peace) and her favorite ball. Her crate is in your car if you need it, but really, if you have to walk her back down to the lot to put her in her crate, you know deep down you're just going to get in the car with her and drive home. These people, this job, aren't worth it.

You blink at the overhead florescent lights and this all feels so weird. You remember this place, but it feels like another lifetime ago. You and Molly Jones ride the elevator to the fifth floor, make your way to the time clock, slide your badge through, and find your desk. The calendar still says March 2020 and there's a layer of dust on the keyboard. It's surreal.

"There you are!" your boss says in an overloud voice and you turn to see the tiny man with the too-wide tie who hired you a million years ago. "And this must be Molly!"

"Molly *Jones,*" you murmur, and you bend down to shush her, because she's begun growling in the back of her throat like she does every time she perceives a threat, like a bird flying too close to the window or thunder. "It's okay, girl," you say, voice filled with fake cheer. "We're okay. This is, um . . . Bossy. Say hi to Bossy, Molly Jones!"

Molly Jones does. Her leash breaks free from your grip as she lunges, jumping up and sinking her teeth into your boss's startled face, tearing into an eye socket with ferocity. Blood spurts and your boss is screaming as he stumbles and falls backward. Molly Jones snaps again, sinking her teeth into his lip this time and ripping, shaking the swath of flesh in her jaw before she drops it to bite off his nose.

"Oh my! You're eating his face!" you say, delighted. She's so clever, solving your little "return to the office" problem in one fell swoop.

Molly Jones stops for a moment and looks at you, head cocked the side, your boss's severed nose between her teeth.

"Good girl," you say. Because Molly Jones is, in fact, the cutest, smartest, most loveable dog in the world, just as you've known all along.

GIBTOWN

Chloe Suresh could taste the dust and heat in the air as she stepped out of her Mini Cooper.

"You drive a clown car! How appropriate," the old man on the porch exclaimed.

Sure, like I haven't heard that a million times. Gets 35 miles per gallon, though, doesn't it? She tried to brush away her annoyance, offering the man what she hoped was a bright smile. She was here in Gibtown on assignment from the *Sarasota Bee*, ordered to interview as many people as she could in this retirement community of sideshow performers. On the anniversary of his disappearance, the paper hoped to uncover new clues in the decades-old mystery of whatever had become of carnival showman Gavin Gilman.

Problem was, she couldn't really *tell* any of the carnies why she was here.

"My aunt's ex-boyfriend was a sideshow freak," Andrew had said when Chloe came home and announced the story assignment. "I can probably get you in touch with him."

"Why haven't you mentioned this before?" Chloe asked, surprised.

"Aunt Teddy dating Frankie the Two-Faced Man isn't something we normally brag about at family reunions," her fiancé had said with a shrug. "But I wouldn't lead with the whole Gavin Gilman thing. Mom asked Frankie about it once, and he looked like she'd just dropped Mentos in his Diet Coke. Called Gilman a no-good sackless bully, and the world was a brighter, better place without him. You could tell it *really* chapped his backside when she mentioned him."

So when Chloe had finally connected with the artist formerly known as Frankie the Two-Faced Man, she hadn't mentioned Gilman, simply claiming she was writing an article on retired carnies. Frankie had sounded pleasant and perhaps even doddering on the phone, and agreed to give her an interview. Eyeing the slightly stooped seventy-something leaning hard on the porch rail now, she found it hard to believe he was even capable of getting worked up about anything, much less his long-gone former boss. Frankie was currently offering a goofy grin and a half wave. Guiding the conversation to Gilman's disappearance would be a piece of cake.

She surreptitiously studied him as she climbed the steps to shake hands. He looked perfectly normal, like someone's grandpa. Thinning wisps of white hair framed a lightly freckled scalp; in fact, the only thing confirming his supposedly colorful past was a sleeve of tattoos lacing one arm, disappearing under his faded Oxford sleeve. A small smile teased the corner of her mouth: among the illustrations in the black and blue ink, she spotted the Punisher logo, a Grateful Dead dancing bear, and what looked to be a rather amateurish and not-at-all wholesome depiction of Hello Kitty in a bikini.

"Thanks for agreeing to meet with me, Mr. Garrett," she said.

"Pshaw. Call me Francis, please. Well? Shall we get it over with? I'm sure you're dying to see it."

Chloe raised an eyebrow. She *was* curious to see the feature that had given him his moniker, but good heavens, she didn't want to be rude. Had he caught her eyeballing him? She started to protest any such interest, but he held up a palm to cut her off. "C'mon, now. Better to see it up front then let it fester in your imagination 'til you won't be able to think 'bout anything *but*." He jerked up his shirt, and there it was: Francis Garrett's second face.

One lid was closed, a seam of skin in an otherwise smooth, if liver-spotted, pale belly. The other eye, however: that's where the horror really began. It was wide open, clouded like a cataract, yet blankly staring at her, as if judging Chloe for wanting to ogle it, and finding her lacking in moral character. Beneath the seam of a lid and the milky eye was a prehensile nose, a ridge of cartilage pressing up from beneath the skin as if struggling to break through. Indeed, two small slits that Chloe presumed to be nostrils *had* broken through, as well as a thin gash with rough, reddish flesh on either side, suggesting a mouth. She let out a small yelp of alarm when the nostrils flared, as if indignant at her gawping.

Francis chuckled, letting his shirt drop. Chloe laughed nervously, at once almost weepily grateful the man had relieved her of the sight. "Parasitic twin," he said. "We share the same lungs, and part of our spine—that's how's I can flex his nostrils like that. Same nervous system. You can't see it, of course, but he's got a mostly fully formed ear under my skin there. I call him Bert. Lemonade?"

Chloe blinked away the image of an ear pressing up against the viscous tissue lining Francis's stomach, as if eavesdropping on what Chloe and the twin's host were saying about it. "What?"

"Something to drink? I've got pink lemonade, or water . . . might have some instant coffee, if you prefer. 'Course, it'll all have something a little extra in it, like dirt." He waved at the warped wooden porch boards covered in a thin layer of filth. "You're here in the dry season. Dust gets in everything this time 'a year."

"I'm fine," she said. She took a deep breath, and could *feel* the grittiness of the air as it moved into her lungs. She coughed. "You know, maybe some water after all. Thank you."

The old man disappeared into the shadows of his doublewide. Chloe settled into one of the porch rockers, waiting for the man who might shed some light on the disappearance of human curio peddler and con artist Gavin Gilman some forty years ago.

Francis set his lemonade on the porch railing. "My parents tried to kill me, you know. It was the doctor attending my birth who convinced them to give me up for adoption. Which, of course, didn't quite work out as planned. Not too many young couples eager to adopt a baby with a second face on its belly."

"*Oooo,*" came a low moan from under Francis's shirt. Chloe's eyes went wide.

"That's right, Bert: nope. Oh, don't mind him. Bert sometimes gets chatty, but he ain't capable of much more than a few sighs or groans once in a while." He patted his side gently; lovingly. "The Sisters of Charity took us in. Taught me my letters and numbers. And occasionally took us orphans out for day trips. Local museums, libraries, and if we were extra good, the fun places. Coney Island was my favorite. That's where I was first introduced to the concept of a sideshow. I knew I'd found my people." A wistful smile played across the man's face.

"I ran away from the sisters when I was sixteen. It was 1958, the country was in a recession, and I'm sure they were happy just to have one less mouth to feed. In any case, I never saw any nuns poking around the Lower Bay askin' questions or tryin' to find me. And that was fine by me. That's where I tied up with Gus Sanders. He ran the sideshow for Robert Moses at Steeplechase Park. I met Hank in my Coney Island days—you know, Howell the Horrifying Wolf Man? Ever heard of him?" Chloe shook her head. "I'll introduce you later. He lives four homes down. Boy, was he a sight to see. Hair from the tippy-top of his scalp to his toes. Auditioned for that *I Was a Teenage Werewolf* movie and was told he didn't look realistic enough. Can you believe it? Old Hank, he still hasn't gotten over that. I wouldn't mention Michael Landon when you meet him." Francis chortled.

Chloe let her mind wander as the old man spoke, her iPhone recording the tale for transcription later. Steeplechase had closed down in '64. Gilman had disappeared in 1978. Francis had over a decade to go before he got to the story she was here for, and he seemed to be taking his time.

"Once Steeplechase shut down, Hank and I set out on our own. We'd heard the real money was in traveling shows. You know, pop-up carnivals in small towns across the country. And sure, it was fine starting in spring and summer, and all those harvest fairs in New England in the fall, but the money dried up from November through May. Unless we wanted to go out to California, which, after Hank's failed screen test, he wasn't inclined to do."

Francis cocked an eyebrow at Chloe. "Ever been to New Orleans for Mardi Gras?"

"No."

"Good for you. Bunch of amateurs, got no right calling it 'carnivale' or whatever. All those masks and beads and boobies. Not that I object to nudity, mind you."

"*Oobs*," Bert added agreeably.

"But it's nothing like a carnival at all! When Hank and I tried our luck there, we were practically driven out of town. Everyone got all shrieky and 'get lost, freaks' when we tried to go shirtless on St. Charles during the parade. It was hot as the dickens, and Hank was practically wearin' a fur coat, for chrissake. Did those naked cretins care? Nope. Chased us down an alley, throwing sticks and beer at us. And not one outfit down there was willing to take on two *genuine* sideshow performers. Only way we got enough money to leave town was we met an old voodoo lady who was willing to pay Hank a nickel an ounce for his back hair."

Chloe couldn't help herself. "Was that when you joined up with Gilman's Tremendous Traveling Show?"

Francis sighed. After a moment, he spoke. "Knew you'd ask about that bastard. Eventually, yes. Around '74, I think. We were still green, you see, and relieved to have a permanent outfit again. We didn't know any better. But it was evident, early on, that Gavin Gilman was a skinflint. He'd make up excuses to withhold wages—docked me one time because Bert was sleeping come show time, and I wouldn't poke him in the eye and wake him up. But it was worse than that. Gilman was a terrible man. Just a horrible, sick . . . *dangerous* excuse for a human being." Francis's jaw clenched, his forearm tightening so as to send a ripple rolling across Hello Kitty's ample bikini bra. A look of such dark, malicious hate clouded his face that a chill spiked across Chloe's skin, making her wonder if *Francis* wasn't the dangerous one, despite his age.

"At first it was little things, red flags here and there that we ignored. Bella the Bearded Lady was sporting a black eye on opening night in Phoenix, the biggest show of the year for us. Then in St. Paul, Tinkalina and Tiny Tom, the midget couple, took off in the middle of the night. Tink was pregnant, see, and Gilman was *mad*. Her legs were all swole and she was throwing up all the time, and she couldn't perform like she used to. They were supposed to be the Leaping Lilliputians, but she couldn't leap no more. Rumor had it Gilman tried to knock the baby right out of her. Tom and Tink were having none of that. They waited 'til the wee hours after opening night, when everyone was good and soused from the post-show celebration and likely in a coma, sleeping off their Mad Dog, and they hauled out of there." Francis paused, reaching for his half-drained lemonade. "She lost the baby just the same, I heard. Don't know if it was 'cause of Gilman or just 'cause she was so tiny. We heard she left Tom for Wee Willie Winkie a couple months later, and old Tom, he wound up just drinking himself to death. Poor little guy."

Chloe leaned closer, picking up her pad to take notes alongside her recorder now that he was on to the good stuff. She'd only found one article in the *Bee* records on Gilman's disappearance, and it hadn't mentioned Gilman's penchant for violence. She'd printed it out, and she glanced at it now to double-check. *Carnival showman Gavin Gilman was reported missing by his wife Merriam on Tuesday,* read the piece dated October 18, 1978. *But authorities believe he may have disappeared months earlier. Visitors to the Tremendous Traveling Show report they haven't seen the colorful sideshow owner since midsummer. One of the earmarks of a Tremendous performance was always the amusingly belligerent Gilman himself, emceeing between each act. Attendees of shows in August and September reported it was Neville the Sword-Swallower who performed between numbers.*

Chloe scanned farther down the article. Yes, there it was: *While most of Gilman's entourage opted not to comment, Bella the Bearded Lady did give a statement: "Gavin Gilman had, above all, a remarkable eye for unusual talent, and an undeniable charm that he turned on every night to get people through the doors, with impressive results. His disappearance is a huge loss to Tremendous, and to the sideshow community as a whole."*

This didn't sound like a man who made enemies wherever he went. He sounded like a successful publicist, and one that Bella was sorry to see disappear. "Are you sure? I mean, this is the first I've heard of . . ." Francis's angry scowl made her jerk back a bit, holding up the yellow legal pad to her chest like a shield. "Sorry. Go on."

"Gilman was a grade-A prick, okay? Cheap and mean and twisted as hell. When Erik the Giant died—peacefully in his sleep, the lucky fool, though he was only thirty, so maybe not so lucky after all—Gilman had his bones boiled and bleached, then charged people a dollar a head to look at the skeleton. No respect for the dead, that man.

"For all that Gavin tried to short us our wages and make us work for free, though, me and Hank, we managed to save a few coins here and there. We had it set in our minds we'd work for Tremendous only as long as we had to, and not a minute more. Talked about opening up our own show, maybe getting in at those state fairs that wouldn't have Gilman back again on account of his temper. I think we could'a done it, too. Been all right."

"Why didn't you, then? What happened?"

"Hank went and fell himself in love."

Francis began slowly rocking in his chair, eyes drooping. Chloe wondered if he was settling in for a nap, or worse: maybe having a stroke right here in front of her. She waited, watching his lids sink lower and lower. Did Bert sleep when Francis did? How did that work, exactly? But no, Francis had said Bert dozed off before a show. Perhaps their napping schedules were independent of each other.

A loud snore emanated from Francis's belly, ruffling his shirt. Francis jerked awake. "Sorry 'bout that, little lady. Sometimes when he goes down, he likes to try and take me with him. Where were we?"

"Hank fell in love," Chloe said, maybe a little too fast.

"Oh. Right. Well, Mitzi couldn't exactly up and leave Gilman's outfit, and Hank wasn't leaving Mitzi. So we stuck with Tremendous 'til Gilman got himself disappeared. After that, we hooked up with a few more shows, but really, by the late seventies, the writing was on the wall. Wasn't much of a market left, what with all those hippie liberals demanding equal rights for little people and protesters deciding 'sideshow freak' wasn't PC anymore, without stopping for a minute to think to ask *us* how we felt about it. Made people feel guilty about seeing us perform, and drove us right out of business. So Bert and I gave up. Got a job with the state as a prison guard, put in my twenty-five years, and retired here." He waved an arm, as if the trailer park they were now sitting in was a grand estate to show off. "Lots of us did. C'mon. I'll introduce you to some folks."

"B-but . . . wait. What happened to Gilman?"

"Darned if I know," Francis said, struggling to his feet. Another loud bleat from his midsection, and he blushed. "That was Bert. It wasn't a fart. Just so we're clear."

Chloe's eyes narrowed. The disconcerted, red-cheeked look Francis wore as he denied the fart hadn't changed from the one he'd had seconds earlier when he'd denied knowing what had happened to Gilman.

She was pretty sure Frankie the Two-Faced Man was lying on both counts.

Chloe dutifully slowed her pace to match Francis's as they left his place and made their way to the dirt path of the trailer park. "Who's that you got with you, Francis? You're picking 'em younger and younger these days!"

Chloe instinctively returned the smile of the large black woman on the porch of the home they were passing. "Hello," she called out. "I'm Chloe. I'm a reporter." The woman stiffened, smile dropping. "Doing an article on retired carnies and their take on what killed the industry," Chloe finished quickly, hoping it was enough to put the lady at ease.

"Killed the industry?" The woman shot upright, her words a squawk. "I'll tell you what killed it! Celebrities, that's who!"

"Huh? I don't follow."

"Look at me," the woman said, tossing aside the crocheted blanket that had been draped over her legs moments before. She took a few hesitant steps off her porch, clutching the shaky railing tight, and made her way to Chloe and Francis. "See?" She turned sideways to show off her profile.

Chloe's mouth dropped at the protruding hindquarters. Two perfectly rounded, impressively gravity-defying cheeks sat high and proud on the woman's backside.

"This is Adele," Francis said. "She used to go by Hecuba. Ever heard of her? Hecuba the Hottentot? From the wild tribes of Africa? No?"

Chloe shook her head.

"I used to make a fine living showing off my assets," Adele sputtered. "You don't need to tell me: I *know* my butt looks great. Used to be a time when people would pay good money to see an ass like this in a G-string. But now? Thanks to the Kardashians, everyone and their mother can buy the Adele Addison look. Nothing special about me anymore." Tears threatened to spill from Adele's baby blues.

"Except yours is all natural, Dellie." Francis gave her left cheek a friendly pat. "Can't put a price tag on that."

"You smooth talker, you," Adele practically cooed, the tears suddenly gone. "Stop by my place later, and maybe I'll let you do a little mountain climbing."

Francis winked.

Chloe cleared her throat. "I'm sorry. What's a Hottentot?"

Adele turned her crystal gaze back to Chloe. "Oh, honey, that's just a word some barker came up with ages ago to describe black folk who didn't look like everyone else. Believe me, it sells a lot more tickets if you claim to have a wild African Hottentot behind the curtain instead of old Bronx-born-and-raised Dellie Addison."

"Good point," Chloe said thoughtfully. "So you think that's it? The death of the sideshow is the Kardashians' fault?"

"Don't be ridiculous," Adele scoffed. "Wasn't just them. Started back when those wrestling folks put an actual giant in the ring. Who's gonna pay a dollar to see a carnival giant—which, let's be honest, after Erik died, was really just Neville on a pair of stilts—when they can watch André on television every Saturday morning for free? Accompanied by a pair of hoochie-coochie girls? Wrestling stole *all* their best acts from the sideshow: clowns, snake charmers, warriors with painted faces, origins unknown . . . no, I don't just blame the Kardashians. I blame Vince McMahon."

Chloe opened her mouth to reply, then closed it again. She didn't know much about wrestling, but even *she* had heard of André the Giant, though she was pretty sure he'd died right around the time she was born. She decided to try a different tack. "What about Gavin Gilman? Do you think his disappearance hurt the sideshow industry at all?"

Adele folded her large, fleshy arms across her chest. "I think it *helped* the industry. And if you don't mind, I'd appreciate it if you never mentioned that worm's name again in my presence." She spun on her heel, stomped up the steps without so much as a glance at the handrail this time, and marched through her front door, slamming it shut.

"Oops," Chloe said.

"You'll have more luck getting the show folk to talk to you if you don't mention Gavin," Francis said, his tone chilly in the August humidity.

"*Uurr oss.*"

"Well, look who's up! That's right, Bert. Gavin Gilman was a gen-u-ine turd blossom." Francis's whole demeanor changed, like the sun breaking through clouds. "C'mon. Let's go see if Hank's around."

Instead of a doublewide, Hank Delazanos lived in a small cape tucked between the trailers. "Hank's done all right for himself," Francis explained before Chloe had a chance to ask.

The old man rapped lightly on the doorframe before opening the door and strolling in. "Hank? Mitzi? We're not catching you two in a compromising position, are we?"

"We're in here," a lilting, breathy voice called out.

Francis nodded, gesturing to Chloe. "Living room. In the back." He moved down the hallway with purpose.

In the bright, air-conditioned room, on a plush red couch crowded with decorative yellow pillows, sat a glossy-skulled man in a faded, sleeveless Florida Panthers tee and boxer shorts. Behind him, balancing on the back of the couch, sat a woman with blue-silver hair teased into a bouffant, not a strand out of place. Her eyes, a green so deep they rivaled the lush rolling fields of Ireland, should have been her most striking feature. But Chloe was unable to tear her eyes away from the woman's skirt—or, to put a finer point on it, the absence of legs below it. The legless beauty was carefully applying a strip of blue fabric to the back of the man's neck, without so much as a wobble from her precarious perch.

Francis cleared his throat. "Chloe Suresh, meet Mitzi and Hank Delazanos. Formerly known as Howell the Horrifying Wolf Man and Loretta the Legless Wonder."

"I'm sorry—what?" She blinked at the man on the couch, who was at that moment scratching a remarkably smooth armpit. "Are you pulling a joke or something? I mean, forgive me, but I've seen newborns with more hair."

Hank let out a laugh, a deep roaring bellow that shook his whole frame and the pillows on the couch, though Mitzi didn't teeter in the slightest. A *twuuch!* cut off Hank's mirth with a flinch as Mitzi pulled the blue strip from his neck.

Oh. He's getting waxed!

"Francis didn't tell you how I made my fortune?" the Wolf Man asked.

"No." She glanced at Francis.

"Hank here is the proud inventor of the Waxing Moon Practically Painless Hair Removal System." Francis offered his friend a toothy grin, which the man mirrored in response. Hank's canines appeared to be filed into sharp points. *I don't care if he's hairless. That's still creepy*, Chloe decided.

"Got the wax formula patented and everything," Hank said. "Though it was Mitzi who suggested we add the 'practically' in the title."

Mitzi yanked away another swath of fabric. Hank winced. "With good reason," he added.

Chloe was familiar with Waxing Moon—had used it herself, in fact. "I love that brand," she admitted. "And it *does* tend to last longer than getting a wax at the salon. How'd you do it? Come up with the formula, I mean?"

"Wasn't easy," Hank said with a sigh. He leaned back, and Mitzi set aside the strips of fabric and pot of wax, folding her arms atop Hank's head and resting her chin there.

She's probably heard this story a million times, Chloe thought, not without sympathy. But she *was* curious. Waxing Moon was impressive stuff.

"As you might imagine, hair removal has been something of a passion of mine since . . . oh, probably around the time I started shaving, in kindergarten." Hank rubbed his chin. "Even back then, when the other boys were blowing up frogs with firecrackers, I was locked in my room with my science kit, trying to find a way to get rid of my shaggy pelt. Not that I had much choice. Dad kept me locked up pretty much *all* the time."

Mitzi leaned forward and kissed Hank atop his head. "Poor boy," she murmured.

"Nah. It was fine. I've always been a bit of an introvert. Once Dad sold me to Gus Sanders, though, I had to put my science experiments aside and get used to being the center of attention. Not that I hadn't been whenever I stepped outside, but this time, the reaction was more positive. When you *pay* to see a wolf man, then by golly, you're darn happy when you actually *see* one."

Chloe was having a hard time reconciling her smooth-skinned narrator with any sort of werewolf. Only the pointed canines that occasionally flashed as he spoke belied his carnie days.

"I didn't have much need to work on any sort of hair removal formula when I was with Gus," Hank went on. "I *liked* being Howell. But things change. Coney Island went under, and Francis and I eventually found ourselves tied up with Tremendous. Then I met my gal Mitzi." He looked upward, offering a wink. Though she couldn't possibly have seen it, Mitzi patted his head in reply.

"Started caring a little more about my appearance. I mean, sure, I needed to keep my face and chest furry for the show, but I didn't need to be shaggy all over, if you catch my drift."

Chloe squirmed. She was pretty sure he was talking about waxing some sensitive spots, which she'd rather not think of in association with this old geezer. Oh God. She'd always assumed the Waxing Moon name was referring to the howling wolf picture on the jar, but what if . . . ? She slid a hand to her own backside before she could stop herself.

"Yup, there too," Hank said with a chuckle. Chloe tried to shake the image of Hank Delazanos's hirsute hindquarters from her mind.

Failed.

Mercifully, he started speaking again. "So I picked up some supplies here and there as we traveled with the show. Started experimenting again, testing out different concoctions. Wasn't all roses and supple skin, neither." He held up a flip-flop-clad foot, and Chloe spotted for the first time a deep, scarred pit in the meat of the big toe. "This was just one of my failed attempts. Shouldn't have added that bottle I picked up from the witch doctor in New Orleans—turned out to be silver nitrate. Ate right through my skin down to the bone in a matter of seconds. Hoo, did that burn! I should've gone to the hospital, but that bastard Gavin wouldn't let me off for the night. Had to hobble through my bit same as always, and then the cheap prick docked me half my wages 'cause I couldn't crouch down just right to howl at the moon, on account of all the pain."

It was Mitzi, not Francis or Hank, who reacted to the mention of Gilman's name this time, and Chloe was thankful she hadn't been the one to bring him up. The legless beauty suddenly looked old and pinched, and most of all . . . scared.

"But I eventually got it," Hank quickly continued, perhaps sensing his wife curdling behind him. "Just the right blend of brown sugar, lemon juice, and lye. And my secret ingredient, of course. Which is going to stay that way."

"Plus coconut oil," Francis said.

"Yup. That was my gal's idea," Hank said, beaming. "Add a little scent to make it appeal to the ladies." He reached a hand above him, and Mitzi took it with a small smile. "I'd be lost without this fine specimen of a woman. That's the thing, you know. Being a sideshow curiosity, well, you'd think it'd be a lonely life. But me and Mitzi, we found our family among those freaks. We'd be nowhere without our friends."

No one spoke, the hum of the belabored air conditioner providing symphony to the moment of shared comradery.

"It's hypertrichosis," Mitzi finally said.

"Beg pardon?" Chloe asked.

"What Hank has. It's a rare genetic disorder. That's what *most* of us have," she added, lifting a thigh and pulling back her skirt to reveal a sudden stump. "Phocomelia for me. To sum it up, I suppose, a sideshow is mostly made up of folks with bad genes. And more than a few unscrupulous liars," she added with a giggle.

"I wouldn't call them *bad*, so much. A few of us did all right with our faulty genes," Francis said, bristling. He gave his side a comforting pat. "I can't imagine how ordinary—and lonely—my life woulda been without Bert."

"Point taken," Mitzi said with a nod.

"And you two lovebirds wouldn't have this fancy shack if not for Hank's hypertrichosis. Waxing Moon paid for this palace. I wouldn't say that's bad genetics. That's a pretty happy luck of the draw, I'd argue."

"Calm down now, Francis," Hank said. "You're right, of course. But Mitzi is, too. I don't know that if I'd had my say in it, I would've asked to be born a freak. But we've made the best of it."

"And now you have your own little house on the prairie," Chloe said brightly.

A thundercloud crossed Hank's face.

"How dare you mention that show? That *man*? Out! Out of my house!" he roared. He jumped up, grabbed Chloe's shoulders with two powerful paws, and spun her toward the door. Trembling, she scampered for the exit, hearing Francis apologize behind her.

"She's just a kid. She don't know no better."

Outside, she took two deep breaths to calm herself, then found herself choking on the gritty air once again. Francis approached her, shaking his head.

"What just happened?" she gasped out between coughs.

"I told you not to bring up Michael Landon," he said.

"I didn't! I don't even know who that *is*," she protested.

"Well, aside from stealing that teenage werewolf role out from under Hank's nose, he also starred on *Little House on the Prairie*."

"Darn it! I knew that phrase sounded familiar," she said.

"Good job, kid. Gonna take Mitzi all afternoon to settle him down again."

"I'm sorry," Chloe apologized again as they approached Francis's trailer. "I didn't kno—who lives *there*?" She stopped, pointing to a bright pink mobile home two lots down. There was a wheelchair van in front, and a second car advertising the

Hillsborough County Visiting Nurses Center on its side. A handicap ramp led from the parking spots to a door that appeared to have not one, but three deadbolts. The windows were latticed with iron bars.

"That's Bella's place," Francis said.

"*Ell*," Bert confirmed.

"The bearded lady? Can I meet her?" Chloe hadn't learned a single thing about Gavin Gilman's disappearance in the hours since she'd arrived. She found it ironic that she was now looking at writing an article about the very lie she'd first fed Francis: the colorful lives of retired sideshow performers.

"No, that's not a good idea," Francis said with a sad shake of the head. "Bella's not in her right mind anymore. She's pushing ninety, you know. Got the dementia." He tapped the side of his head to emphasize the point. "I might have some pictures, though. From the old days. Would that help?"

She smiled, nodding, and Francis headed up his steps. She paused for one last look at the bearded lady's fortress before following.

"Might take me a few minutes," Francis called out from somewhere farther inside the trailer. "Never been much good at organizing. Teddy was always on me about that—say, how is your fiancé's aunt, anyway?"

"She's, uh, dead," Chloe said from her seat at the kitchen table. "Sorry. Breast cancer—about two years ago."

Francis appeared in the doorway, holding a dented shoebox. "Well, ain't that a kick in the pants. I sure am sorry to hear it. Breast cancer. That's rough. She had dynamite knockers, too."

An image of Alex's Aunt Teddy came to Chloe's mind, belting out Stevie Nicks at karaoke night the last time the couple had visited her in Atlanta. *Dynamite knockers. Teddy would've liked that,* she decided. "You found the pictures? Thanks. This'll really bring the article to life."

Francis set the box on the table, then slid a chair next to her. "Here's one of me and Bert, back at Coney Island. We sure was a handsome pair, huh?" Chloe snapped a shot of the Polaroid with her iPhone, then studied it. A teenaged Francis was standing on the boardwalk, shirtless, strawberry blond hair ruffling in the breeze, his chin tilted at the camera. Bert's gossamer eye seemed to be staring right at the camera, and his slit of a mouth was slightly upturned, suggesting a smile.

"You look happy," she said. "You both do."

"Those were happier times," Francis said with a shrug. "Here. Take a gander at Hank." He handed her another photo.

Two charcoal eyes peeked out from a field of dark, coarse hair covering every inch of Hank's face. His shaggy arms were held up as if ready to grab the photographer, his sharpened canines displayed in a menacing grimace. If not for those teeth, Chloe didn't think she would've recognized him in a million years.

"That was a publicity shot, I think. He really was something."

"He should be using *this* to advertise Waxing Moon," Chloe said. "He's got the ultimate before and after shots here."

"Hmm. That's not a bad idea."

"Think I could ask him to pose for an 'after' shot for the article?"

"Let's give him a little while to get over your ichael-May andon-Lay misstep," Francis advised. "C'mon. There's got to be a picture of Bella in here somewhere."

Chloe plucked a handful of images out of the box and started sifting through them. She paused occasionally to snap a photo. A towering man who was unmistakably Erik the Giant. A tiny couple, beaming next to a regular-sized minister, who Chloe assumed were Tinkalina and Tom. She spotted Hank again, arm in arm with two other performers, and snapped it with her phone before peering more closely. An olive-skinned woman, perhaps of Middle Eastern descent, grinned widely at the camera. Her beard was magnificent. "Is this Bella?"

"You found her!" Francis clapped. "Ain't she a knockout?"

But it was the woman behind the trio that captured Chloe's attention. She sat sidesaddle on a white horse, facing the camera, and both beauty and beast were adorned with peacock plumes. Her long, blonde hair cascaded down to her waist. One finger coquettishly touched her lips, and between her crossed legs, draping hair, and feathers, it was impossible to tell if she were clothed beneath the plumage. "She's beautiful," Chloe said. "Who *is* that?"

Francis squinted at the picture, then frowned. "Merriam. Gilman's wife."

"Really? What did she do?"

"She was a hoochie-coochie girl. You know: rode the horses, held the snakes, whatever. Danced between numbers at the show. She wasn't a stripper, if that's what you're thinking," he added when Chloe's eyebrows lifted. "She was a class act. But it was her job to get the marks in the door."

"Is she around? Can I talk to her?" Maybe there was a chance to save her original story after all.

"No." The word shot from Francis like a bullet. "Merriam's long gone."

Dusk was just starting to reach its shady tendrils across the sky when Chloe retreated to her car after thanking Francis profusely for his time. She sat behind the wheel for a minute, staring at the pink trailer with the ramp. While the other retired performers she'd met had all made it quite clear they felt the world was a better place without Gavin Gilman in it, Bella had been the one quoted in the article as saying Gavin's disappearance was a loss. Why?

She *really* wanted a few minutes with the bearded lady.

Chloe drove to the outskirts of town, and settled in to wait for night to fully fall. She shot Andrew a text saying she wouldn't be home 'til late. Then she tapped *play* on her recorder app.

She learned nothing new from listening to what Francis and Hank had said. She jotted down *hypertrichosis* and *phocomelia* when she heard them again in Mitzi's breathless voice, then brought up Google images. She found several examples of hypertrichosis, and learned it was rare and incurable. Of the ten or so cases she found online, all looked similar to the pictures of Hank in his youth, and all had gone on to careers as sideshow attractions.

The phocomelia photos were more unsettling. There were several images of infants and toddlers with malformed arms and legs, underdeveloped facial features, and fused fingers and toes. None of them looked like Mitzi, however. The distorted limbs either ended with stunted hands and feet—some missing digits—or tapered off where the limb hadn't finished growing.

But Mitzi's thighs hadn't shown signs of missing bones or gnarled, fused balls of flesh. They looked more like the stumps of shark attack victims or amputees.

Mitzi hadn't been born that way. Why had she lied?

Chloe started her engine and headed back down the road. The retirees of sound mind in Gibtown weren't willing to give her answers. Maybe the woman with a few loose marbles would have a loose tongue, too.

She parked on the side of the road about a block down from the dirt drive leading to the carnie community. The almost-full moon provided enough visibility that she was confident she wouldn't walk into any trees, though she stepped gingerly to avoid rocks and holes along the path. She lingered at the mouth of the road that opened wide to the array of trailers. The crickets hushed at her arrival, but their chirring picked up again after several seconds. A subdued glow cut through the shadows from somewhere inside the Bearded Lady's pink palace. *Oh, good. Looks like she might be up.* Chloe fought the urge to run across the open lawn and up Bella's ramp.

She kept to the edge of the clearing as she wove her way over. A quick glance to the left told her Francis had likely turned in for the night; his place was dark. She kept her steps soft as she crept around to the back of the pink trailer, where she found a second, shorter ramp leading to a deck. The curtains were a blushing red, like undercooked meat, and half open across the sliding glass doors cutting off the patio from the inside.

Chloe drummed the glass with her nails, then waited, listening. Nothing. She realized she'd been holding her breath. *Of course nobody's coming. You could barely hear your own tapping over the crickets!* She tried again, using her knuckles this time, but gently.

Nothing.

A third time. Movement inside.

Light splashed across the deck, and Chloe silently cursed. She hoped Francis was asleep, or he'd surely see it. A figure rolled up to the window, skeleton-like and clad in a thin pink robe, frayed at the cuffs. "Barbara?" A tinny voice whispered, the click of one lock, then a second, being turned.

"Yes, it's me," Chloe lied. She'd be whomever this old woman wanted, if it got her the story. The glass door inched open.

Chloe stepped inside, wincing when another light snapped on, this one from an oil lamp on a table near the patio doors. The acrid scent of burning dust filled the room.

Bella the Bearded Lady peered up at Chloe from beneath wiry white eyebrows and a cap of tight curls. The skin on her cheeks was yellowed parchment, the tip of her nose almost translucent blue, but all was overshadowed by a glossy white beard that traveled down her jowls and across her chin, curling to a point where neckline met chest.

Her beard was still magnificent.

"I'm so, so sorry to come here like this, so late, but you see, it's an—"

"Barbara! It *is* you!" Bella's eyes lit up. "Come, sit. You must tell me all about your new gentleman friend. George, is it? The detective? Let me put water on for tea. I'm so glad you're here!" Rolling backward to give Chloe room, Bella motioned to a chair at the oil-lamp table. "Sit!"

Like an obedient dog, Chloe sat. "I-I don't need tea. Listen . . ." she didn't know if Barbara was a family member or friend. She studied the frail bird in the wheelchair across from her. Should Chloe call this woman Grandma or Bella? What if the moniker was a stage name, like everyone else she'd met that day? If Bella's real name was Gertrude or something, the jig would be up. She glanced about the room. The only frame on the wall held a portrait of a portly man, blond hair cropped in a buzz cut, wearing a salesman's smile that didn't quite reach his cold gray eyes. *Gavin?* Chloe cleared her throat, returning her gaze to Bella. "Listen. It's about George."

"He proposed!" Bella clapped her bony hands like an excited child. "I knew it!"

"No, no, not yet." Ideas were churning in her mind, quickly flashing like cue cards, only to be tossed aside for a fresh draw. She decided to take a chance. "George has been asking questions. About Gavin."

"Oh." Bella's shoulders slumped. She shuddered, and a moment later when she held out a shaky palm across the table, Chloe took it gently. Her fingers were icy to the touch. Chloe began rubbing the old woman's hands between her own, instinctively trying to pass on some of her own body heat. "Oh."

"I'm sorry. I just . . . I don't know what to tell him."

"Well, you can't. You can't say anything. It had to be done. You know." A single, fat tear tracked a slow descent down Bella's cheek, disappearing into the white wilderness of her beard.

"I know," Chloe said. Then paused. "Why, again?"

"You know I don't abide by cheating. Men have needs, of course; they can't help themselves. But it wasn't right, what

Merriam did. She made a vow afore God and the rest of us to be faithful to her husband. If she'd just kept her legs closed—oh. I'm so sorry." Bella pulled her palm away to cover her face with her hands. "That was uncalled for, I know."

Chloe waited. Bella slowly pulled her trembling hands from her face, looking at Chloe with wet eyes. "Barbara!" Her face lit up. "When did you get here?"

"She was just leaving." Francis stepped over the runners of the sliding door, the butt of his pistol tapping the glass as he pushed it wider.

Chloe shot from her chair, pulling herself tall. "I am *not*. I've had it with you people and your mysterious 'he just disappeared' bullshit. Tell me what happened to Gavin Gilman, or I'm going to make up something ten times as awful as what probably really did happen."

Francis regarded her with black eyes. "Unlikely."

Chloe let her gaze drop to his gun, which Francis held low at his waist, trained on her. She forced herself to meet his steely glare again. "Bella said Gavin's wife cheated. Did she kill him? To get out of the marriage, maybe?"

A second figure ducked through the doors. "*I* killed him," Hank said.

She turned to the hairless wolf man, startled. "You? Why?"

Francis half turned to look at his friend. "Hey, now. Give the boys their due. Bert and I helped."

Hank smiled. "You did."

"Thank you." Francis gave the man a satisfied nod, then faced Chloe again. "We had to."

"Yes, Bella mentioned that. Why?"

Hank sighed, letting his head droop, and for the first time since she'd met him Chloe could see the weary old man in him.

How old *was* he? Seventy? Eighty? Older?

"Gavin was a taskmaster, and heavy with his fists—Bella, you remember. I seem to recall he showed you the back side of his hand a time or two."

"I loved him," Bella announced.

"You did not, you silly old fool. A couple of tumbles in the hay when you were both stewed to the gills does not a romance make," Francis sniped.

Hank shot Francis a warning glare and moved over behind Bella to rest a palm on her shoulder. "We know you did, baby. But he was no good for you. For any of us."

Bella sniffled.

"Our bearded friend here hasn't had an easy time of it. Her father left when she was a child, and once Bella hit puberty and her stubble started coming in, her mother kept her locked in a room in the basement. Gave her nothing but cat food and water to live on. When her mom died—car accident, and she was an Iranian woman in a foreign land, no friends or relatives in the area to speak of—it was two weeks before the landlord found young Bella, starving and covered in her own excrement in that basement closet. I hate how she lives now, all the bars, the locks, right back where she started, it seems. But we have to keep her *in*, you see. Or the truth will get *out*."

Chloe gave Hank a quizzical look.

"Because she's nuttier than a pecan log and can't keep her yap shut!" Francis said, leaning in to shout the last words at Bella, who flinched.

"Stop that, Francis. Bella can't help her situation. At least she's happy here, and loved." He gave the bearded lady a sad smile, then looked at Chloe. "You can imagine why, when Gavin found her on the streets hooking a year or so after she was found in the closet, and brought her to Tremendous, our beautiful Bella regarded him as something of a knight in shining armor." Hank rubbed Bella's arm. "He was likely the first person in her life who'd ever shown her anything resembling kindness, even though he treated her no better than the pimp who sold her out to johns by the hour on the street. But he kept her fed, and gave her a place to call home, and gave her a tumble once in a while."

The old woman sighed. "You remember, Barbara, don't you? How he'd give you a coin for cotton candy from time to time?" Bella winked at Chloe. "He knew what a sweet tooth you had."

Hank shook his head sadly. "Yeah, that never happened. That man never parted with a nickel unless he was getting something worth at least six cents in return. Listen, we all knew our boss was a mean piece of work. But we didn't know what he was capable of. The cold-blooded cruelty. Until he caught me and Mitzi one night behind the Tilt-a-Whirl at the Portland Polka Festival."

Chloe blinked. "Mitzi? But why would he care?" She looked at Francis.

"Mitzi's a nickname for Merriam, you pudding head," he said.

The realization of what Francis was suggesting took hold of Chloe, throwing coils around her mind and threatening to squeeze it to bursting. "No." The word was a whisper. "He couldn't have—"

"He could and did," Hank murmured. "We were going to run away together that very night, but Gavin, that snake, he must've known exactly what we were planning. Dragged Mitzi by the hair back to their trailer, then locked himself in with her.

Oh, how she screamed! My heart broke a thousand times that night, hearing those howls, like a wounded animal begging for death. And I couldn't get to her to save her. I tried."

"We all did," Francis added. "He'd pulled the dresser across the door to barricade it, and the strongman's barbells to boot."

"I still hear her screams some nights," Bella said, her eyes unfocused. "Though I *do* think by the time he started sawing off the other leg, she'd passed out."

"She had." Hank gave Bella a reassuring pat on the shoulder.

Chloe's stomach churned. She couldn't imagine a man—a *monster*—doing such a thing, and to his own wife? It was unthinkable. "So he . . . did that to her. Cut off her legs."

"Yes." Hank's brow furrowed. "We couldn't let him live. You see that, right?"

The words stuck like butterless toast in Chloe's throat. She let her chin drop in a nod instead.

"We waited until the Memphis show. Hardest two weeks of my life, seeing him preen like a rooster, thinking he'd got the best of Mitzi and me . . . *proud* of the way he'd mutilated her. I wanted to choke that smirk right off his face. But we had to wait."

Chloe found her spit again. "For what?" she rasped.

"We needed time to make enough Waxing Moon," Francis said.

"I don't follow."

"Version six-point-oh, or whatever batch it was. The one that ate the hole in Hank's toe." Francis stabbed a finger toward Hank's slippered foot.

"I kept notes rivaling Einstein when I was working on my experiments. Wrote down every concoction I tried," Hank said proudly. "That one was no good for hair removal. But it did a fine job of reducing flesh and bone to slurry, should the occasion call for it."

"And this one did," Francis said.

Bella lifted a hand to tap the one Hank still rested on her shoulder. "Careful, now. Barbara says George has been asking questions."

"Pinhead Barbie died yea—"

"Hush, Francis. Don't be cruel." Hank settled a look plump with sorrow on his friend.

Chloe started. "What? Wait, she thinks I'm a pin—I'm micro—I'm one of those people with a little head?" She instinctively ran her palm over her ponytail. "Well, that's certainly humbling."

Hank's tone was even as he settled his gaze back to Chloe. "By the time we hit Memphis, we had two full tubs' worth of the stuff. And there was no way I was going to wait even a minute longer. In the meantime, Bella here was the one tending to Mitzi's wounds, holding her hand through the nightmares. Memorizing little messages from me to give my girl."

"My memory was a bit better then," Bella agreed. "Those were dark times. I don't care how handsome Gavin was—what he did wasn't right. Barbara!" Her eyes lit up. "When did you get here?"

"Hush, now, Bella." Hank suppressed a smile when Chloe twisted her fingers through her ponytail again. "So when we were ready, our bearded friend here invited Gavin to her camper and slipped him a mickey."

"I did good?" Again, the old woman reminded Chloe of a child.

"You did good, honey," Hank said lovingly. "Once he passed out, Francis and I carried him to our trailer. We borrowed Nigel's handcuffs—"

"I thought Nigel was the sword swallower?" Chloe interjected.

Francis shrugged. "He was. Bit into the kinky stuff, Nigel was. Don't interrupt. It's rude." He glowered at her, rubbing the nose of his gun across his Punisher tattoo.

"Anyway. I was so mad, you see, I couldn't do it myself. I needed Francis there to keep me focused. We couldn't afford to be sloppy, or we'd get caught. Once we had Gavin secured, I slapped him awake. Oh, was he ornery when he came to and found himself staring at me instead of Bella's five o'clock shadow!" Hank chuckled. "He was cussing and threatening to cut *my* legs off, and my johnson, too. He didn't have much to say for long, though."

Francis leaned in. "It was Bert's idea to cut Gavin's tongue out first."

"*Ung,*" came the moan from underneath Francis's shirt.

"Yup, and a fine idea it was, too. What'd we use for that, Francis? Pliers?"

"Hedge clippers, I think," Francis said, scratching his chin.

"You're right. We snipped that right off, and dumped it in the tub of Waxing Moon six-point-oh we had waiting right under the table. Really helped with the screaming, too, once the tongue was out. Sounded more like barking after that."

Chloe swallowed hard. "I don't think I need to hear any more of this," she said. She felt like a shrimpy kid on the playground, except here the big kids were pummeling her with horrible sights, over and over until she just wanted to curl up in a ball and cry.

"I think you do," Francis said, folding his arms across his chest, the gun still tightly gripped in one hand. "Go on, Hank."

"We cut off his fingers, one by one. Then his toes. He was yowling as much as he could, and crying, and I'm pretty sure he was trying to say 'please.' That was something, hearing the big boss man begging for us to go easy on him after what he'd done to my girl. I wasn't having any of it. Like *he* deserved mercy." Hank's lip twitched up, revealing a glistening canine. His eyes were those of a wolf, disconnected from all but the cold hunger for payback.

"So we cut strips of flesh off his calves and his thighs, and whenever he'd pass out from the pain, Francis would pour whiskey over all that exposed fat and tissue and wake him up right quick again."

Francis chuckled. "Never met a man who deserved it more."

"I cut off his nose next, then carved out an eye. Kept one in, though, and made him watch when I took off his arms at the elbow with an axe."

The sour tang of bile burned in Chloe's throat. She swallowed it down. "Please. I see. No more," she said weakly.

"Not much more to tell, really. We chopped him up and melted his body parts down to sludge. Eventually, when I was good and tired and had my fill, we fed him a jar of six-point-oh. I think that's about what finished him off, isn't it, Francis?"

"Pretty sure," Francis agreed.

"*Uurr oss,*" Bert said.

"That's right, buddy. We murdered the boss," Francis said, affection in his voice.

"I loved him!" Bella shouted again.

"Loved who, Bella?" Hank's fingers dug into the old woman's shoulder a little deeper. His grinned, a horrible smile of grotesque fangs.

"George?" the woman said hopefully.

"Sure you did," he replied, and gave her shoulder one last squeeze.

"I think I do need that tea now," Chloe said, unable to quell the tremble in her voice. She wanted to shake the picture of a skinned Gavin Gilman from her mind. She thought of the beautiful blonde with the scintillating peacock feathers and the legs that went on forever, and the matronly, perfectly balanced legless woman with the striking silver bouffant she'd met earlier today.

Gavin Gilman had been murdered by his sideshow freaks. It was without a doubt the story of a lifetime.

Chloe Suresh would not be able to write it.

ANDY WARHOL IS MY WINGMAN

"You know, they say Andy Warhol died a virgin."

Merrill and Vanessa stood in front of a series of Campbell's Soup cans hanging brightly on an alabaster wall. Merrill wasn't sure how he should respond: he and Vanessa had met online only a week ago, and this was their first date. It was she who'd suggested they meet at the Museum of Modern Art; Merrill would've preferred a bar, or even Starbucks, but he wanted to please this girl. She'd been the only one after two months on Tinder who seemed the slightest bit interested in seeing him naked.

He decided to play it safe. "Mmm."

"Mmm-mmm good!" She punched his arm playfully. "You're funny!"

The joke was unintentional, but if he'd just scored a point, he'd take it. "You hungry? There was a sign for a café . . ."

Vanessa nodded, and they fell in step toward Terrace 5. Merrill cocked his head. Was she . . . *humming*?

"Mmmmm."

Yeah, she's humming.

"MmmmmoMA. MoMA. Mow-mah."

She's a freak, he decided.

"Ever notice how words seem to lose all meaning if you say them over and over?" she said.

"Technically, MoMA isn't really even a word."

Vanessa stopped short, sneakers squeaking on the linoleum floor. "Seriously?"

He shrugged. "Um, yeah. It's an abbreviation, not a word."

"No, I mean, are you *seriously* going to be like every other nitpicky smeg out there, getting on my case, being all 'MoMA's not a word'—what are you, the grammar police?" She crossed her arms, frowning.

He put up his hands, palms out, the universal sign of surrender. "Hey, I didn't mean anything by it. Just making conversation. Listen, I'm nervous. It's our first date, I don't want to say something stupid—too late, I know—and I'm starving. Sorry, okay?"

Her face softened into a smile. "Yeah, okay. I get it. That's sweet." She snaked an arm through his, resuming their stroll to the café.

It was the third time she'd taken him off guard. The first, upon meeting outside the museum doors, was when he'd inadvertently cocked an eyebrow at the sight of her fanny pack. Vanessa wasn't bad to look at—big green eyes, snub nose, D cups big enough to cause the buttons on her blouse to strain— but a *fanny pack*? He hadn't seen one of those since his mom had taken him to the Grand Canyon back in 1995.

She'd seen the brow shoot up and set her shoulders back. "Say what you will—they're handy as all git-out."

"I'm not saying a thing," he'd said, and winked. But he could tell from her stiffened neck she wasn't pleased.

When they'd gone to get their tickets, he'd pulled out his AAA card for the $7 discount—after all, he lived outside the city, owned a car, and the insurance and discounts AAA offered were handy—she'd nearly pitched a fit. "What're you *doing*?" she'd asked, as if he'd just whipped out his junk and peed on one of the decorative plants in the lobby.

"I, uh . . ."

"I'm not *worth* paying full *price*?"

"No! I mean, you are—I just—" he'd glanced at the heavyset black woman dressed in tomato orange manning the ticket booth. She shook her head in sympathy, quirking *her* eyebrow. "Forget the discount," he'd muttered, forking over his debit card.

"Sure you want to go through with this?" the ticket woman murmured, and he'd nodded resignedly. "Your funeral." The tomato slid their admission stubs over the counter.

And then Vanessa had insisted on paying him for her ticket, not more than three seconds later. He debated asking what the hell the point of that snit fit had been. *I do* not *get this girl.* But still, if she put out at the end . . . he let it go.

They found their way to the café, sitting at a turquoise-topped table next to a wall-length window overlooking the city. He flipped over the menu, skimmed it, and smiled.

She returned his grin. "Find something good? What're you having?"

He paused a moment, scanning his memory to see if she'd mentioned being a vegan in any of their texts. No, he distinctly remembered her sending a selfie posing with a slice of pepperoni.

"Filet mignon and scallops."

Storm clouds drew across her face. "Are you *kidding* me right now?"

"What?"

"You *know* how I feel about Steve Irwin."

He did—they'd had a conversation about their favorite celebrities, and she'd enthused over the Crocodile Hunter to the point of embarrassment. But—steak and scallops—he didn't follow.

"Huh?"

Tears pooled in her eyes. "Scallops. Most restaurants don't serve actual scallops, you know. Of course you do—we've talked about this!"

They had not. She was absolutely, unequivocally, nuttier than a fruit bat. He sat, waiting.

"They're—they're—scooped from rays, you insensitive bonehead!" She was full-on sobbing now, her nose running, her cheeks blotchy and pink. She hunched forward, presumably to dig a tissue out of her belly bag, and he caught a glimpse of fleshy cleavage and . . . was that a Care Bears tattoo? *You're seeing things,* he told himself. *It's a Grateful Dead dancing bear for sure.* Except he could see a little stormcloud on the belly of the blue beast. It was absolutely a tattoo of a rather childish Sunday morning cartoon from the eighties.

He stared at the cartoon bear peeking out from her left breast. Considered what it might be like to stroke it. "You know what? I don't need to know," he mused aloud.

"You *do* need to know. Steve Irwin was a saint, I tell you! You know he legit walked on water, right? I sent you that YouTube link—"

"No." Merrill's chair scraped as he pushed back hastily. "Not. One. More. Word. I'm out." And with that, he fled, leaving Vanessa blinking at the space he'd just occupied, half-open belly bag on her lap.

He sprinted down three flights of stairs before slowing, certain she couldn't catch up, then exited the stairwell in favor of a corridor. He thumbed up his Tinder app on the phone and blocked Vanessa's profile, then did the same with her phone number in his contacts list. He glanced up to find he was back at the Technicolor soup cans.

"Sorry, Andy. Looks like you and me are both dying virgins." He studied the silent silkscreen.

Did a double-take.

Tomato, the printing read on the can.

"You're right. Thanks, buddy." With that, Merrill resumed his sprint. He might still be able to catch the tomato at the ticket counter before her shift ended, and see how *she* felt about going out to Starbucks or a local bar.

ACKNOWLEDGMENTS

Usually in this section of the collection, the author thanks their agent, editors, beta readers, publicists, and the members of their writers' group. I have no intention of doing any such thing, mostly because the people I'm about to mention also served in some capacity as any of the job titles I just listed.

I chose the title *Tempered Glass* for this collection after facing a pretty serious and utterly unexpected diagnosis that was a *lot* to deal with. I wanted the title to be a reminder that much like the titular noun, when heat and pressure are applied, I, too, am four times stronger than regular glass. Maybe even more. Who knew I had it in me?

I would not have had the mental strength to focus on anything, much less such a time-consuming project, without endless cheerleading and love from my family on both the best and worst days: Mom, Dad, Kim, Tim, Nathan, Evan, Auntie Bea, Auntie Joan, Lori, the Ross and Smith families . . . I'm so thankful for all of you. I love you.

I need to also thank some friends, who are all pretty darn great: Rachel, Jen, James, and Renee, for starters. Thanks for keeping me sane. The rest of my EB family, my writer family . . . there are just too many of you to name, but you know who you are. Thanks for having my back.

Even an editor (which I am sometimes) needs an editor, and I'm lucky enough to have one among my friends. Thank you to Adrian Vladimir for helping out on this one. I'm in your debt.

When contemplating whom to beg for an introduction, my first and only choice was Tony Tremblay. Besides having the rightful moniker "The Nicest Guy in Horror," he's simply one of the best human beings I know, and a talented writer to boot. I'm so lucky to have him in my life.

I also knew immediately whom I wanted for a cover artist. Stephanie Johnson did the cover of my first collection ten years ago, and I thought it would be fitting and wonderful to have her again. I surfed on over to SLJohnsonimages.com to make sure she was still in the "making magic happen" business (she was), then reached out. The result was the work of art that adorns this tome. Thank you, Stephanie. I salute your brilliance yet again.

A side note: when reading through stories to select what to include in this, I realized that I sure do like to throw in identical twins as supporting characters. It should come as no surprise to anyone to learn that when I was a young 'un, I counted a set of identical twins among my closest friends. While I must stress that none of the twins in any of the these are meant to be Amy and Melissa, who are both delightful and lovely people, I must also thank them (or maybe apologize to them) for allowing me to use their twinness in so many tales.

Finally, and probably most importantly, this collection would not have been possible without the encouragement, help, support, and unconditional love of Matt, the love of my life. You and Maggie make life pretty darn wonderful.

Stacey Longo is the award-winning author of *Ordinary Boy*, *Secret Things*, *My Mom Has MS*, and *My Mom, MS, and a Sixth-Grade Mess* (winner of the Preditors & Editors Readers' Choice Award for Best YA Novel of 2017). Most recently, her YA mystery *My Sister the Zombie* was released by The Storyside Press to much fanfare and celebration, at least in the author's mind.

Visit her online at www.staceylongo.com.